SEEKERS
OF THE
STONEHEART

An Illustrated Novel
by
Kurt and Tyler Librandi

A MAP OF
CYNORRUM
Mount Zearus
Elbrith
Lilum
The Green Vails
The Terric Ocean
Nymm
Haroon
MUKKIS
Mandoril
Blackwater Swamp
Gomer
Feverwood forest
Dwyn
Weeping Meadow
Cliffs of Jagurak
Marsh of Lear
Rook
GRAVEEN
Anura
Village
The Sleeping Sea
Aramore
Noakwood
Hollow
Mogoroth
Larkindale
Echo

Wravik
Listening Lake
HAVARRIA
Gammon
The Wraithwood
BANN-GAR
Weavergutt
Kazum
Lake of Lament
Tavet Ruins
The Scar
Vinum's Port
JENOHA
Wicknott
The Rolling Dunes
The Raging Sea
Ralore
Qwelm
PYRUS
Talon mountians
Dacarr
The Ablens
Hoven

Summary: When Arden's secret—a blue stone embedded in his chest—is exposed, he becomes the target of a deadly hunt. Forced to flee, he seeks a witch in Blackwater Swamp, only to uncover dark truths about his past.

Librandi Publishing
Printed in the U.S.A
First Edition, March 2025

Acknowledgements

To the incredible editors and beta readers—Stephen M. B., Sabrina Iraggi, Brittnie Cole, Addison Riccoboni, Nasser Dagdag, Julia Alberigo, Adriana Estrella, and Nicholas Mattheus Villamil—your time, insight, and thoughtful feedback have been invaluable in shaping this story. The authors are deeply grateful for your contributions.

A special thank you to Gina Melton, whose guidance and encouragement helped ignite the authors' creative ambitions. Your belief in them has meant more than you know.

And finally, to Bill and Linda Librandi—your unwavering support, love, and wisdom have shaped not only this journey but also the people the authors strive to become. Your influence is woven into every page, and for that, they are forever grateful.

CHAPTERS

SEEKERS
OF THE
STONEHEART

Chapter 1
THE THIEF FROM THE WOODS

Arden had no memory of how he ended up by the river eleven years ago nor of the event that had left him wounded. He could recall his name, but nothing more—not his family, not his friends, and especially not the origin of the mysterious stone embedded in his chest.

On many nights, he'd gaze upon the stone's misty blue surface, wondering how it came to be. He'd never seen such an odd rock in all his life. And though it was rather beautiful, Arden was more concerned with the pink scar surrounding it. He loathed the wound's appearance—even the thought of it was enough to make him cringe.

No one can ever know about it, he often thought. *No one ever should.*

Arden was determined to keep his stone a secret. It was already bad enough that he was a thief, despised by his fellow Elves in the neighboring forest town of Aramore. They offered him no compassion—no acceptance—and the same bitterness was extended to his adoptive father, Gord.

Life was rough for them both—Gord, "the bloodthirsty Ogre," and Arden, "the thief from the woods." They were outcasts, feared and hated. But Gord always reminded his son that they didn't need acceptance from the Elves. They had each other, and *that* was all that mattered.

Arden tried to heed his father's words, but it was difficult to look past their hardships. True, Gord had provided a roof over his head, and it was also true that if Gord had never found him all those years ago by the river, the boy would've been left to die. Yet still, Arden longed for more. He wanted to live a life full of luxury, like many Elves did.

Stealing things was Arden's closest way of gaining what he yearned for—the one thing he *did* have control over—and he was incredibly skilled at it, too.

For most of his fifteen years, Arden had learned to slip through cracks and vanish like smoke, honing his talents as a master thief. He could stand behind a bush and no one would even know he was there. It wasn't just his woods-like appearance—messy and wild—but his ability to become one with his surroundings.

Gord, however, disapproved of his son's thievery—despite being the one who had taught him to steal as a child. Back then, times were different. Survival demanded it, and the Ogre had only trained the boy to take what was necessary.

But Arden had grown to love the thrill, the excitement of taking what wasn't his.

Today was no different.

Arden had just pulled off another theft, succumbing to the urge as if it were an itch that needed to be scratched. Not a soul had caught a glimpse of the boy as he fled Aramore. Another flawless escape, as always, except for a minor scratch on his leg. Granted, leaving the scene without an injury was preferable, but the fast-healing boy didn't mind.

Radiating with pride, Arden returned to his hilltop home in Noakwood Hollow. The forest's towering trees stood like guardians of time. Sunlight filtered through their canopy of emerald leaves, casting golden patches on the woodland floor. Moss-covered trunks whispered secrets, their rustling leaves singing a tranquil melody as Arden envisioned the riches awaiting him from his stolen spoils.

This is it! he thought.

His life was about to change, perhaps for the better, because today, he had stolen something of true value: a necklace made of genuine pearls.

Arden grinned as he emerged onto the crest of the hill. Taking a few steps up, his gaze was drawn to the sight of his humble abode in the hollow.

Unlike the spacious houses in Aramore, Arden's was... *unique*. His home was carved into a giant acorn that had fallen from the first noakwood tree hundreds of years ago. Perched atop the hill, this odd dwelling stood as an ancient relic of the past, a seedling that fate had kept forever young. A single round window was carved into a knot beside the crooked front door, and the cottage's sides were overgrown with clumps of moss.

The house had always been a bitter yet comforting sight for Arden after a grueling day, even if it was just a single room. But this time, as the boy drew closer, his steps wavered. A chill ran down his spine as a putrid scent filled the air.

A tower of smoke swirled out of the acorn's stem chimney. Gord must have been cooking.

Keen to remain unnoticed, Arden quickly crouched down and tried to stay out of sight. He carefully crept up the stone steps and stretched his head toward the door, which Gord had left open just a crack.

Silence filled the house, except for the bubbling of a pot. Arden peeked through a bit further.

CHOMP!

The boy glanced to the left. Gord stood by the counter, his back turned and bald green head glistening with sweat. His massive hand flew high into view, clutching a jagged stone knife.

Its blade reflected the last gleams of daylight onto Arden's face.

Then, the Ogre brought the weapon down with brutal strength. The countertop shook, and an unsettling sound echoed through the air like bones breaking.

Although Arden couldn't see the butchery, he could hear his father's heavy footsteps shuffling across the room. With a splash, Gord dropped something plump into their ceramic cooking pot.

Arden rubbed his chin as an idea took shape, a mischievous grin spreading across his face. He reached into the satchel tucked beneath his green cloak, careful to remain silent. From within the bag, he drew a slingshot crafted out of sticks and vines.

With the weapon in hand, Arden knelt on the steps and snatched a rock that had chipped off one of the stone tiles. He rolled it in his fingers, determining if it would be of adequate weight. The rock was dense and jagged, perfect for grabbing Gord's attention.

Arden pressed it against the sling's band, pulled it back toward his pointed ear, and then—

SMACK!

The pebble flew across the room and whacked into the wrinkly folds of the Ogre's neck.

Gord froze, dropping the knife to the counter. The dull clang of the stone blade sang throughout their acorn cottage.

Arden waited, glaring at the back of his father's bumpy head.

In an instant, Gord's bloodshot eyes locked onto the boy.

"Hey!" Arden shouted, lowering his slingshot. "Quit leaving the door open, Gord. You're letting all the flies in, especially with *your* cooking."

Where have you been? the mute Ogre signed with a few gestures of his hands.

Arden smirked, then said aloud, "Oh, here and there."

Gord rolled his leaking eyes, then stomped over to the pot hanging above the fireplace and tossed in some vegetables. Seconds later, a smell worse than rotten garlic overtook the house.

Arden held his nose. "Again with the druff root, Gord? You know how much I hate it. And just look at what it's doing to your eyes."

The boy walked inside and dropped his satchel and cloak by a wobbly table near the fireplace.

The sound of the fallen bag awoke a small creature resting atop a leaf nest in the room's corner. It was Mugz, Arden's pet mugget: a strange little beast with floppy ears and a long tail. Her beady black eyes remained unseen behind her massive, furry brow, but her wide grin showed pure excitement.

Mugz barked happily, scampering over to nuzzle Arden's legs.

"I know, Mugz. I know," he said, patting the creature's horns. "I'm glad to be home, too."

Arden walked over to a mirror and studied his long, dark curls, carefully adjusting the leaves in his hair. Then he sat on his straw bed and removed his shoes as Gord set the table.

Gord grabbed three wooden bowls from the dusty shelves of a cupboard and poured the foul-smelling stew into each. He set them in their usual places: one on the floor for Mugz and two on the table for himself and Arden.

Gord sat down, tucking a rag into his collar. He snapped his fingers, signaling for the boy to eat his dinner.

Arden sighed. "Just a second, Gord."

The boy stowed his shoes under the bed and joined his Ogre guardian at the table.

Gord's soup looked disgusting as always, thick clumps of druff root floating atop a sea of brown sludge. Delightful.

"Gets thicker every time," he muttered, attempting to remove his spoon from the gunk.

Gord huffed, then signed, *You waited too long.*

Arden wrestled with his utensil, twisting and pulling, but it was no use. The spoon clung stubbornly to the bowl as it fused to it. Gritting his teeth, he tightened his grip and gave one fierce yank. Suddenly, the spoon broke free, launching out of the soup and clattering onto the floor.

Gord rolled his eyes but offered to help. He leaned from his chair and reached for the utensil. As he grabbed the spoon, a sparkle from within Arden's satchel caught his eye.

"You didn't have to clean that for me," Arden said. "I could have gotten it myself..."

The boy fell silent, and his heart began to race as Gord lifted his head back above the table. The Ogre was now holding a familiar pearl necklace in his hand.

Gord scrunched his face and slammed the table with his fist, jiggling the soup in their bowls.

Mugz quickly scurried under Arden's bed.

"It's not what you think!" he exclaimed.

His father tossed the necklace onto the table.

You disobeyed me again, Gord signed. *That's the third time in a month. I let the bracelet slide by, and even that set of rings, but this is too much. I hope, for our sake, you weren't seen by the guards.*

"N-no, I wasn't," Arden stammered. "And even if I was, those guards would never follow me into the hollow. They think it's haunted... and they're probably too scared of *you.*"

That's not the point, Arden. You know you can't keep doing this.

"But this time is different. That necklace is more valuable than anything I've taken before. It's not a big deal anyway. Those Elves don't need what I've stolen."

So you just get to keep their belongings for yourself, then? Gord asked. I mean, how many times must we go through this? Do you have the slightest idea what would happen if they built up the courage to search these woods for us? They'd kill me and lock you away forever. To the Elves, you're just a criminal, and me, some bloodthirsty monster. They despise us. And stealing from their people just gives them an excuse to hunt us down. We don't need that worry, let alone a bunch of their jewelry.

Arden crossed his arms. "Well, you were the one who taught me how to be such a good thief in the first place. And besides, I wasn't going to keep anything. I'm trading all of it at Mogoroth."

Gord signed, Arden, you're fifteen now. When are you going to learn there's no reason to steal from the Elves anymore? That's in our past. We have all that we need.

Arden paused, torn between Gord's perspective and his own. "Well, what do you expect me to do with this stuff, then?"

Take everything back.

"Everything?" Arden shouted.

Yes. The bracelet, the necklace, the rings. All of it, Gord signed. You'll bring them back tomorrow before we trade at Mogoroth, and I expect no questions.

Arden seethed, tired of always losing these fights with Gord. Just then, something within him snapped, and rage bled through the boy like never before.

"No!" he finally protested, snatching the necklace back

into his grip. "This stuff will help us, I know it. Lake Stillwater has barely provided enough fish for us to eat, let alone any to trade at the market. If I sell these items, we'll be set for months."

Arden, you have to learn to appreciate—

"No! Don't start that again. I don't have to do anything. Everyone else gets to have whatever they want. And us? We have to eat the same thing, day in and day out. Well, maybe you can do it, but I can't. I want more; different foods, new clothes, a proper bed with real sheets. I don't want to live like this anymore, like a..."

Arden's fists curled.

Like what? Gord signed.

"Like some freak!" the boy choked, sinking deeply into his chair, tears beginning to well in his eyes.

Gord remained silent for a moment.

Son, you are not a freak, he signed. *None of us are, we're just misunderstood. I know you want better for us, but the things we have are more than enough if we just learn to be grateful for them. We are lucky for this roof over our heads, the warm fire, and the food to fill our stomachs. Not everyone can say that. Stop being so stubborn and learn to appreciate what you have right here in this room.*

Arden couldn't bear another word. As much as he hated their living situation, his father was probably right. He *should* be grateful. After all, it was Gord who, above everyone else, provided for him in times of need and struggle.

Arden's tears simmered, and he nodded to his father across the table.

Good, Gord signed. *Now, swear to me, you'll bring that jewelry back. You'll feel much better if you do the right thing.*

Arden glanced away but muttered, "Fine."

Chapter 2

THE BLACK MARKET

At the first light of dawn, Gord rose earlier than usual to prepare for a day of trading at Mogoroth, the black market. He carefully filled a large bag with various items: sickle and gloon fish, ferry tongue leaves and rupp fruits.

Even Mugz chipped in, offering a helping paw. Crawling out of her snug leaf nest, she pulled a cluster of muttleberries from a nearby vine and carried them to the Ogre in her small, sharp teeth.

Gord accepted the mugget's weekly contribution, adding the berries to his bag before hoisting it onto his massive shoulder. With everything ready, he made his way to his son's bedside, the final task on his morning checklist.

With a hefty nudge, Gord shook his son awake.

Arden flung his eyes open abruptly and pushed his father's hand away.

"Alright, alright!" he groaned. "I'm up!"

I got our supplies packed for Mogoroth, the Ogre signed to the half-lidded Elf. *Mugz and I will wait outside for you. Don't be long.*

Arden rolled over, letting out a deep yawn as his father and Mugz left the house. Blinking away the remnants of sleep, he slowly sat up and stared at his legs, trying to shake off his hazy focus.

It appeared his cut from the day before had healed, its skin smooth and unblemished.

Finally feeling more awake, he swung his feet over the

side of the bed and stood up. With little concern for taming his wild hair or changing his clothes, Arden grabbed his mossy cloak and satchel, threw them on himself, and approached the door.

Before stepping outside, a brilliant glimmer flashed from within his bag. A beam of sunlight illuminated the stolen jewels he'd acquired, catching the boy's eye.

Arden hesitated, biting his lip in contemplation. He was well aware of the moral obligation to obey Gord's demand and return these items, but a nagging doubt clawed at him.

Was that his *only* option?

Arden understood the importance of honesty, and he respected his father's wisdom, but he yearned for more than the meager existence they shared in Noakwood Hollow. Life as an outcast—scraping by on whatever they could find or trade—left him feeling resentful of those who had more, especially the Elves of Aramore.

At that moment, a realization struck the boy. Gord would never condone trading stolen jewels, even if they *were* valuable. But the final decision didn't lie solely with the Ogre. The fate of these trinkets rested in Arden's hands.

Perhaps he could just *pretend* he returned everything. But how difficult would it be to smuggle jewelry into Mogoroth without his father noticing?

The idea began to take shape in Arden's mind. He could discreetly conceal the items beneath his clothing while at Aramore, sell them to the jeweler in Mogoroth, and hide the spoils somewhere Gord would never suspect. Once everything was settled, he could gradually use the money to improve their lives, ensuring the changes were so subtle that his father would barely notice a difference.

Yes, he thought. *It was perfect.*

With newfound confidence, he pushed Gord's wishes aside, sealed his satchel shut, and strode out the door.

As the boy and his family journeyed to the edge of Aramore, Gord watched closely as Arden entered the forest town to fulfill his promise. Tension filled the air as the Ogre waited impatiently. His dark and penetrating eyes never left the path his son had taken, even after the boy had disappeared into the city streets.

When Arden finally returned, he maintained a neutral expression to avoid raising suspicions, but his father wasn't convinced.

Snatching the boy's satchel, Gord rifled through it with rough hands. He thoroughly examined the items inside to make sure the stolen jewels weren't concealed.

Gord paused, shocked that his son had carried out the task. The Ogre's expression shifted to that of reluctant approval, and he gave a firm nod before continuing to lead the way.

Arden and his father trekked back through the dense woods in silence until they emerged at Mogoroth Bay.

The landscape unfolded before them—a vast, glistening expanse of water framed by a thick, untamed forest. The bay sparkled under the midday sun, its calm waves brushing against the muddy shoreline. A salty breeze filled Arden's nostrils as he took in the sight of the black market's entrance, perched above the heart of the cove.

Unlike most cities, which were built of wood or stone, Mogoroth sat within the hollow stomach of an enormous, dead sea monster. Though its preserved body lay entirely submerged, a forest of coral tubes had sprouted from the beast's back, rising proudly above the water's surface like castle towers. From afar, these massive coral structures gleamed with flecks of green and gold, climbing high past the treetops.

Mogoroth would've been a rather extravagant sight if not for the creaky old piers winding from the shore. And it was here that many pirate ships would dock to unload their spoils.

Crooks and merchants alike flooded the port, always lugging their products and loot to and from the market below.

Blending into the crowd naturally, Arden and his family strolled across the piers until they'd arrived at one of the coral towers. Like many of the tubes, this one was hollowed out to make room for a wooden elevator: a Mogo-lift, as the market folk called it.

Passing through the large entryway carved into the coral tower, the boy and his father stepped onto the Mogo-lift's platform inside. As their weight shifted, a small bell chimed, signaling the lift's activation. With a sudden clang, the wooden structure began its slow descent through the hollow tube.

Arden and Gord felt their bodies sway as they were lowered into the depths, the morning sunlight shrinking above them until only a sliver of daylight remained at the entryway.

Mugz, sensing the change, whimpered in fear and nestled herself onto Arden's shoulder.

"Don't worry," he reassured his trembling pet. "It's almost over."

Arden and his father squinted, anticipating the blinding illumination that would soon follow.

As they emerged down into the top of the sea creature's stomach, the city's torchlight burst forth with an orange glow. The sudden transition from total darkness to the brightness of the market below was disorienting.

A sensation followed that was even more unpleasant: a warm, sour stench like that of a million decaying fish. The fleshy innards of the beast had been preserved for thousands of years, yet it still smelled like it had died just days ago.

Gord choked upon the horrid odor.

"Never gets any better, does it?" Arden muttered from behind his clenched teeth.

The Mogo-lift came to an abrupt halt as it thumped to the bottom of the market. Arden and Gord stumbled off the elevator, as they had done many times before.

They proceeded down onto a road scattered with tall and crooked buildings, each one billowing black smoke from their cobble chimneys. Ahead, a familiar sea of patrons and vendors lined the street, their stalls sheltered beneath a mass of colorful tents and overhangs.

As usual, Arden's eyes were drawn to the left, where a familiar Noamin merchant often stood. The small, bearded man enthusiastically spoke about a special hair-growing ointment. Yet, not a single person seemed interested—not even other Noamins passing by, which was odd since Noamins loved growing their beards to great lengths.

Arden couldn't help but feel a twinge of sympathy for the persistent vendor.

On the right, the boy noticed another familiar figure: a small Haggart with messy black hair and blue skin. She was energetically promoting her collection of old books, each one seemingly more boring than the last. Her voice rose above the crowd as she recited excerpts no one would ever want to read themselves.

Arden stifled a chuckle, wondering if she'd ever sold a single volume.

Determined to avoid any unwanted attention, Arden drew his gaze forward once more, avoiding eye contact with other vendors. Each one seemed poised to pounce, ready to lure him into buying their goods with practiced pitches and exaggerated promises.

Eventually, the boy and his father arrived at their favorite shop, The Squib, a large building that sat at an intersection on the main road.

Gord had walked in first, but Arden hesitated, a bead of sweat dripping down his forehead.

"Hey!" he said to the Ogre. "You go in without me."

Gord paused in The Squib's doorway, turning to face the boy with a furrowed brow.

Arden tried to portray some confidence in his tone despite his nervousness, but his tongue felt as dry as sandpaper. He knew this was his only chance to sell the stolen goods to the jeweler of Mogoroth, but he needed a good enough excuse to leave.

The first thing that came to Arden's mind was his Noamin friend, who owned a small gem shop in the marketplace.

"What?" he asked. "I'm going to see Finn. I'm curious to know how his trip to Larkindale went. It's been a while since I've paid him a visit."

Gord began to rub the tiny hairs on his chin.

Seems alright with me, he finally signed.

Arden could hardly contain his excitement. Though he felt a twinge of guilt for lying to his father, he couldn't afford to let it show.

Are you sure you'll be alright going by yourself? Gord signed.

"Pfft! I'll be fine," Arden said, waving a hand. "And don't worry, I won't get conned by any vendors again. I know how to deal with them now."

Arden grabbed Mugz off his shoulder and placed her onto Gord's.

"Here," he said. "She can stay with you."

The Ogre gazed at the boy curiously.

"I don't want her to wander off like last time."

Gord nodded.

We'll be waiting here when you get back, he signed.

Mugz barked eagerly, ready to enter The Squib.

Just be careful, Gord finished.

"I will," Arden replied.

The boy merrily strolled back to the main path, following it briefly before turning down a side street. He had been through this alleyway a few years back and recalled that the renowned jeweler's shop was just at its end.

This street was darker and more secluded, shrouded in an eerie silence that made his footsteps seem unusually loud.

The few vendors that dwelled in this alleyway differed from those on the bustling main road—less pushy, their eyes cold as they silently displayed their wares. Other residents lingered in the shadows, staring at Arden from dark corners and doorways. Their presence was unsettling, like ghostly apparitions studying his every move with silent judgment.

Arden quickened his pace, trying to shake off the feeling of being watched.

Finally reaching the end of the road, Arden spotted a tent covered in green coral ahead. A big sign dangled from the shop's overhang, reading "Big Fish's Trinkets and Jewelry."

An enormous green Tetran vendor stood behind the tall counter, his blubbery frame swallowing more than half the stand. The scent of his fishy scales lingered in the damp air. Like all Tetrans, a prominent set of fins jutted from atop his head, and a heaping mass of warts grew beneath his many chins.

Composing himself, Arden took a deep breath and discreetly removed his left shoe. There, wrapped around his ankle, were the stolen necklace and bracelet. Adorning his toes were the three rings.

Placing all the items in his hands, Arden marched to the Tetran's shop, boldly tossed them onto the counter, and asked, "Hey, how much can I get for these?"

The Tetran appeared engrossed, peering intently into an oversized looking glass, studying a pair of earrings laid out on the table before him. Their gleam caught the light, casting bright reflections onto his purple vest.

"Hello?" the boy asked, his confidence wavering.

For a moment, the Tetran's yellow eyes flew up at Arden, then over to the boy's items.

"I'll give ya a thousand chip," he grumbled, shifting his attention back to the magnifier.

"One thousand chip?" Arden asked. "For all of this? No way! This stuff is worth at least six thousand."

"Six thousand? Ha!" the man laughed, continuing to evaluate his earrings. "Not here, they're not."

Arden tensed.

"Come on!" he protested. "I know these are valuable. They have to be, especially this pearl necklace."

The Tetran finally ceased inspecting his trinkets and pushed his looking glass aside. His eyes narrowed.

"Two thousand chip, that's it," he growled, leaning back on his stool. "If you don't like it, take ya knickknacks somewhere else and see how far ya get. I'm the only jeweler left in this place. Ya won't find anythin' better, kid. I can guarantee it."

Arden's frustration boiled, and he threw all of the jewelry back into his satchel.

"Fine! Whatever. You can keep your two thousand chip. I don't need it, anyway."

The boy stormed off, his rage simmering to discontent. Unfortunately, he *did* need that money, but it seemed this stubborn Tetran wouldn't budge, not for someone like him, anyway. With that, Arden walked back into the alleyway, his disappointment growing as he trekked down the road.

Suddenly, a voice yelled, "Ay! Come back here!"

Arden turned.

"Let me see those again," the fish-man demanded, waving a hand toward himself.

Arden gazed at the vendor suspiciously.

"Don't be so uptight, kid. Bring 'em over," the man said in a condescending tone.

Was this some sort of trick, or was this vendor going to make him a better offer?

Reluctantly, Arden strolled back over to the Tetran's shop and dropped the jewelry onto the counter. The man quickly snatched up the items with his webbed hands. Arden listened as the vendor muttered to himself, rolling the pearls of the necklace in his palms.

Unexpectedly, the Tetran hacked up every drop of saliva he could muster and projected it onto the necklace. Arden recoiled in disgust. The vendor wiped the green-tinted spit over the pearls with his cloak, and they began to shine brighter than before. The slimy man repositioned his looking glass and peered into the magnifier to assess the trinkets one last time.

"Three thousand," he declared. "I'll give ya three thousand, but that's it."

Arden contemplated the offer. Was it only worth that much?

He sighed, placing out a palm for a handshake. "Deal."

The man ignored the boy's gesture, throwing the bracelet and rings into a basket. Then he dropped a bag of three thousand chip onto the counter beside himself and picked up the necklace once more to marvel at its beauty.

"Thanks," Arden said, but as he reached for the bag, a slippery hand slapped his arm away.

"Ay! Wait a second," the merchant snarled. "Where did ya say ya got this necklace again?"

The boy hesitated. "From Aramore. Why?"

The jeweler squinted, and a low growl rumbled deep within his throat. "Stay right there."

He reached down under the counter and grabbed a glass jar filled with a strange blue liquid. It was clear but glowing, like bioluminescent algae from the deep sea.

"What is that?" Arden asked.

The Tetran remained silent as he held the necklace above the jar. Without hesitation, he dropped it into the elixir.

Arden watched intently as the necklace sank to the bottom of the bottle, the pearls gleaming softly in the dim light. All at once, the necklace began to sizzle as bubbles hissed from each pearl, creating a thick foam that swiftly rose to the surface. A bitter scent filled the air, prickling Arden's nostrils. The bubbles swirled and churned, obscuring the pearls in a frenzy of movement. Then, as abruptly as it had started, the fizzing stopped, and the necklace had vanished.

Arden's jaw dropped.

The fins atop the vendor's head began to curl tightly, and his blue face turned a shade brighter than crimson.

"Ya sold me fake pearls!" he wailed.

In one swift motion, the Tetran threw his fists at Arden's cloak and grabbed him by the collar. The boy's face went pale as he felt his legs leave the floor. The enraged Tetran hoisted him into the air, rendering the boy nearly speechless.

"I-I didn't know!" Arden stammered, his voice trembling.

"Liar!" the Tetran thundered. "Do ya have any idea who I am? I'm the big fish of this town. My ancestors built this market from the seafloor up!"

Arden squirmed and struggled, but the fish-man's vice-like grip was unrelenting, his fingers like stone clamps. The boy frantically darted his gaze around the tent, searching for a way out. Then he spotted it: the jar of elixir resting on the countertop.

"Just wait till I feed ya to the laughin' leeches. Then you'll see what happens when ya mess with me!" the jeweler hissed, pulling the boy in closer. "Nobody crosses Big—"

SPLASH!

Arden poured the jar of blue acid onto the Tetran's arm, and a horrifying scream filled the air. Big Fish dropped the boy to the floor and reached over to clutch his burning shoulder. Arden slammed to the ground but quickly scampered to his feet and sprinted for the main road. His heart pounded in his ears, drowning out the hollers of the Tetran vendor.

With haste, the boy threw himself toward the street, knocking over a group of Noamins who had been going about their business. Their top-heavy bodies fell to the floor like beetles rolling on their backs. Their angry jeers and complaints mattered little as Arden regained his balance and charged ahead, his sole focus on reaching his father.

As he turned the corner, he spotted Gord and Mugz leaving The Squib with a bag of fresh food.

"Gord!" the boy shouted, watching his father glance around the street in confusion until, finally, their stares met. Arden felt a sense of relief wash over him as he neared the safety of his Ogre guardian.

He was just a couple of shops away when he felt the familiar grip of slippery hands catch his hood and yank him backward. Arden tumbled to the ground, his head smacking against the floor. Disoriented, the boy struggled to regain his bearings.

When his vision cleared, there stood Big Fish, looming above him with rage. Gord dropped his bag of food to the floor in horror, witnessing everything from afar as the nearby market folk began to spread out, encircling the boy from all sides to watch the scene.

Arden turned to face the vile Tetran, only to see the man's boiling stare warp into pure shock. In the vendor's hands were Arden's shirt and cloak. The brute had ripped them clean off.

Big Fish dropped the clothing to the ground and took a few timid steps backward, his eyes wide with awe as he looked down at the boy.

Silence fell over the bystanders. Then whispers and murmurs rippled through the crowd as they gazed at Arden's chest.

"What is it?" they asked each other. "It's revolting!"

Trembling with fear, Arden began to realize what they spoke of. He peered down at his torso. There, exposed for everyone to see, was the mysterious stone in his chest.

CHAPTER 3

RUMORS IN THE EAST

It was a waking nightmare. Arden's secret was out, his stone glinting over the eyes of three dozen market folk.

Flooded by panic, the boy hastily snatched his clothes from the ground, draped them loosely over himself, and bolted straight for his father.

"Gord! Get to the lift!" Arden shouted.

Now drained of color, the Ogre hurried in compliance. With swift determination, he sprinted to an empty Mogolift down the road, Mugz clinging to his shoulder. Reaching the platform, he drew a stone knife from his belt, prepared to sever the elevator's rope as Arden drew near.

"Cut it!" the boy yelled as he sped through the gawking crowd.

Gord's hand trembled, but with a surge of determination, he brought the knife down in a swift motion. The rope split cleanly, and the sharp screech of pulleys snapping echoed loudly through the air.

Arden leaped high to grab the platform, barely catching its edge as it raced upward.

With a desperate lunge, Gord pulled his dangling son up to safety.

As Arden and his family gained their footing, the gleaming torchlight of the city disappeared beneath them while they sped up into the darkness of the coral tower. The lift quaked and swayed, banging against the walls as the sound of wind whooshed around them. Faster and faster they went, deep into the black. For a few seconds, it seemed as though the hollow tube was endless until—

BOOM!

The Mogo-lift's wooden frame came to a rapid halt, slamming into the top of the tower's entrance.

Hurled like rag dolls, Arden and his father tumbled off the platform. They lay still for a moment, eyes wide with shock. Battered and dazed, they slowly pushed themselves up and fled the scene without looking back.

By afternoon, they stumbled into their acorn cottage. Mugz scurried into her nest as Arden collapsed at the kitchen counter.

Gord slammed the door with both hands, pressing it tightly. His heavy breaths bounced off the door, blowing through the room.

Arden turned to him with pure fear etched across his face.

"Gord?" he asked.

His father swooped around and glared, large veins popping from his neck.

Arden jumped back, bumping into the counter.

"I know you're angry, b-but it wasn't my fault! That Tetran jeweler melted the necklace. He said it was fake and—"

Gord's eyes widened further, and Arden refrained from uttering another word. The Ogre stomped over, standing above him like a towering storm.

You went and sold that jewelry when I told you not to? he signed.

Arden shrank into himself, emitting a loud gulp.

"Y-yes, I did," he said. "But I never got the chip for them because—"

Gord's massive fist slammed onto the counter. Arden flinched.

I should have known I couldn't trust you to return those items, the Ogre signed.

"I-I'm sorry," Arden pleaded. "I should have known they were fake."

Gord shook his head. *You're not sorry they were fake, Arden. You're sorry you got caught. It's as if you've learned nothing from me. And now, not only have you branded us as criminals in Mogoroth, but your stone was exposed to dozens of people. How could you be so inconsiderate? So foolish?*

Arden hung his head, feeling the sting of shame in his chest. He believed he was making the right choice to help his family. His throat tightened with a lump of guilt and regret. He had let down not only himself but his father as well. And worst of all, the stone in his chest, the one thing he'd kept hidden from everyone, had now been exposed to the prying eyes of countless strangers.

Arden shielded his face with his hair, desperate to hide his emotions, but Gord had already seen the tears welling in his son's eyes. The Ogre's tightened shoulders loosened, slouching back down to his sides.

He knelt on the floor to face the boy eye-to-eye, briefly placing a gentle hand behind his neck.

Arden, I was scared for you, he signed. *You're my only family. I can't lose you. Ever. You have to listen to me when I tell you to do something. Please, don't let that happen again. You're all I have left.*

Gord's eyes welled up, and he embraced Arden with tender arms, washing away the tension between them.

Arden sniffled a bit, wiping the tears from his cheeks as his father held him close.

"So, what happens now?" Arden asked, his voice cracking slightly.

As Gord released the boy, his face went rather grim.

Well, it appears our lives are going to get much more complicated. We can't return to Mogoroth or Aramore any time soon. I fear that nowhere is safe except this house. We will have to stay here until people forget what happened.

Arden's brow furrowed. "How long do you think we can keep that up—hiding here? Months? Years?"

Gord shook his head, completely unsure. He walked over to the kitchen pantry, assessing the dwindling food supply on their dust-covered shelves.

We're almost out of things to eat, he signed. *So, tomorrow, we'll gather as many vegetables as we can from the forest. And as far as meat goes, we can keep fishing at Lake Stillwater. No one ever goes there. We should be safe.*

"Great," Arden said under his breath. "Just when I thought our meals couldn't get any more disgusting."

Gord gave the boy a stern glance, reminding him who got them into this whole mess.

Arden recoiled, then gave a meek nod.

We will do what we have to, Gord signed strictly. *And if that means eating sickle fish for a month, then so be it. Maybe things will get better soon, but until that day comes, you need to do exactly as I tell you.*

The boy shook his head in disappointment but agreed, nonetheless. The least he could do was tolerate some smelly fish for a few weeks.

As the evening wore on, Arden said nothing more. He

kept to himself, gathering his cloak and some thread to repair its torn collar.

While stitching the fabric, his mind wandered, heavy with regret. He wanted nothing more than to turn back time and undo the damage he'd caused, but he simply couldn't. He was certain the market folk were already spinning stories about him—whispering tales of "the Elven freak with the blue stone lodged in his chest." The thought burned inside his mind.

It was too horrifying to guess what might come from all of this, but one thing was for certain: if he were to return to Mogoroth so soon, Big Fish would surely feed him to the laughing leeches.

A shiver ran through Arden's body as he tried to wash the thoughts away. But unbeknownst to him, his greatest fears were materializing.

Rumors of the boy were spreading like wildfire across the land of Cynorrum. The tales even made their way to Dacarr, a secluded kingdom deep within the eastern wastes of Pyrus.

Ten days had passed since the incident at Mogoroth, and it was on this night that the boy's secret had finally reached Lord Zark, the cruel leader of the Dacarri people.

In his castle of reddened stone, the tyrant sat in a massive domed chamber. The orange glow of a fireplace illuminated the many battle scars on his face, accenting the bark armor that encased him like a second skin. Atop his head sat two mighty antlers that protruded through his helm, flaunting his power over all who gazed upon him. He was frightening in every sense of the word.

Zark stared intently at the map of Cynorrum sprawled across his stone table. His mind raced with strategies against the Dacarri traitors who had long plotted his downfall. For years, this fierce band of rebels had grown vengeful of Zark's harsh rule, driven to end his reign of unyielding tyranny.

Amidst the man's plotting, a sudden voice echoed from across the chamber.

"Lord Zark!"

The cruel leader kept his eyes fixed on the map. "Who disturbs me?"

"It's Tull."

A towering woman entered the room. Long black locks cascaded past the two small antlers growing from her head, and a red tattoo was streaked down her lower lip, signifying her status as Commander.

"My deepest apologies, sir," she said, approaching Zark with caution, "but I bring news from the west. The stone has been rediscovered."

Zark's stare flew upward, his steely eyes glinting from the embers of the fireplace. "Where?"

"Mogoroth," Tull replied with a steady voice. "Just ten days ago."

"Impossible," Zark said, peering back down. "The stone has been missing for nearly eleven years and was lost far to the north—nowhere near that peasant market." He waved a hand toward the door. "You've fallen for falsehoods, Tull. Leave my chamber at once with this."

"Sir, a boy carries it, a young Elven thief. They say the stone... sits in his chest."

Zark's brow raised high.

"In his chest?" he repeated.

Tull remained silent.

"What does this stone look like?" he asked.

"They say it is blue, like the sky."

Zark tapped his chin in thought, then arose from his chair as a serious expression washed over his face.

"I think it's best we pay this Elf a visit," he declared. "Tell me, Commander, have there been any sightings of our 'friends' to the north? Do they know of the stone's reappearance?"

"No, sir," Tull said. "There have been no indications of their presence."

"Good. We wouldn't want any of their kind seeking it— that is—if any of them are still alive."

Zark glanced at the map, but this time focused on the location of the black market. "Round up twenty soldiers and our largest bull-pigs. Make sure they're well-equipped with enough supplies and armor to last the journey. We set sail tomorrow for Mogoroth Bay."

"Yes, Lord Zark," Tull replied with a furrowed brow.

She began to exit the chamber but lingered in the door-way. With a twinge of uncertainty in her voice, she turned back toward her leader and said, "Forgive me, sir, but if I may—this all seems like a futile effort. After all, the stone's reappearance *is* just a rumor. Do you truly feel this is the wisest choice for our people?"

Zark's expression flattened. He approached the woman, now speaking face-to-face.

"Are you questioning my authority?" he asked calmly.

"No," Tull answered with hesitation.

"Then we have an understanding. We will follow this path to redemption, and you will not question the decisions I make for Dacarr."

"Of course," Tull said, finally leaving the chamber.

Zark stretched a devious grin across his scarred lips as he spun around and approached the fireplace. Atop its mantle rested a single item Zark had worshiped more than any other treasure he'd collected: an ancient ax once belonging to the mythical king, Borka, the father of all Dacarri.

It was said, "From fire, it was forged. And fire, it still bears." An old branch formed the weapon's twisted handle, and two blades made of salka stone protruded from its top, chipped and riddled with deep crevices from battles passed.

Zark often admired the orange gem that was embedded in the center of its blades.

He lifted the ax from its mount above the fireplace and knelt before the burning hearth.

"I wish only to make you proud, Borka," he prayed, closing his eyes as he clutched the weapon. "Our people have remained in darkness for too long without your light. The time to claim what we are rightfully owed has come. The stone belongs to you, father of Dacarr. Allow me this chance. Grant me the fire of your might. Alight this ax with your fury so I may purge the world of your enemies forever. May your flames show the way. I shall not fail you."

Chapter 4
STRANGERS IN THE FOG

A cool wind swept through Noakwood Hollow, finding its way through the cracks in Arden's front door.

Lying in bed, the boy grew restless, haunted by the events of the past nineteen days. Anxiety gnawed at him ever since his secret had been revealed, making sleep almost impossible. Gord and Mugz, however, appeared to be in a deep slumber, their gentle snores singing through the house.

Arden remained tense as he drifted in and out of sleep. The murmurs of a dream started to take hold, his mind replaying the moment his stone was exposed, the shocked faces of the crowd, and the shame that followed.

The whispers of his nightmare grew louder, wrapping around his thoughts like a heavy fog. It was enough to draw the boy back to consciousness.

Arden jerked awake, beads of sweat trickling down his forehead. He felt as though the walls were closing in on him—the heat becoming almost unbearable. He wiped his brow with a trembling hand as a deep fear built within his core.

I need some fresh air, he thought desperately. *Maybe it'll help clear my head.*

Leaping up from his bed with a nervous sigh, Arden snatched his cloak and stepped out onto the stoop, quietly closing the front door behind him.

The night air was crisp, and the trees rustled gently,

casting long shadows that danced across the ground. The moonlit forest was calm, occasionally interrupted by the soft rustling of leaves. If not for his relentless thoughts, Arden would've found it quite peaceful.

He questioned whether he was being overly concerned or not concerned enough. The constant worrying toyed with his sleep-deprived mind. He couldn't help but overthink every little thing.

Shutting his eyes, Arden took a deep breath.

Suddenly, a strong wind blew through the woods. The hairs on the boy's neck stood up as the powerful gust wailed with a ghostly howl and tore the cloak from his back.

Arden glanced around, curious to see if a storm was approaching. But then, everything fell eerily still. No breeze followed the powerful gust, nor did a single leaf rustle.

How strange, he thought.

Reaching for his cloak, the boy noticed something moving down the hill from the corner of his eye.

In a wide gap of two trees, a pale blue fog began to roll between them. It seemed to move with a mind of its own and slowly rose into a steady wall as if it couldn't dwell any further.

Arden jumped to his feet, transfixed by the sight.

Two white lights rapidly shot out from the haze, like a set of eyes staring without a single blink.

Arden's body began to tingle. He felt like his feet were frozen to the ground, incapable of taking a single step.

Voices of women began to creep out from the fog, filling the air with calm whispers. Some spoke in unison, others out of sync. They muttered and chuckled, snickered, and hissed.

Arden was able to catch a few words.

"Son. My son. Where are you?"

An inexplicable draw pulled the boy toward the soothing calls. The voices coiled around his mind, reaching for his very soul. He wanted to reply, but his lips grew tight as if they were glued with sap.

"Follow. Come to me—to mother," the voices beckoned. "We know who you are. Who you really are. I can show you!"

Arden couldn't pull away. The white eyes appeared to be moving closer with every second, and the rest of the forest faded into darkness.

"Your stone. The stone!" they whispered. "We know its secrets. Follow me. Follow your family."

The voices rattled around in Arden's head, but his fears settled, transforming into a profound peace as if nothing else mattered but their words. Nothing except—

A loud whistling sound cut through the air.

Arden's vision fluttered as the glowing white eyes rapidly dissolved back to the familiar sights of the forest. The voices fled from his mind like wisps of smoke.

He quickly turned around to find the source of the sharp sound. Far in the distance sat his house, where Gord waited at the door, calling the boy to return with another whistle. Surprised and confused, Arden rubbed his eyes, convinced that he had been standing on his stoop the whole time. It seemed he had wandered downhill toward the woods.

The boy glanced back at his father.

"Gord! I'll be right there," he replied.

Taking a final look at the trees, Arden noticed that the strange blue fog had now vanished as well. Dismissing the odd occurrence with uncertainty, he started back up the hill to his house, wondering if the last few minutes had been a figment of his imagination.

As the boy approached the stoop, Gord abruptly blocked the doorway. Arden acknowledged his father's concerned expression with a pause, expecting the man to step aside, but he didn't.

What are you doing out here? he signed. *I woke up and saw you weren't in bed.*

"Oh... It was getting too warm in there. I just needed some fresh air," Arden said.

Gord leaned his head toward the boy, keeping a stern gaze fixed on him, waiting for something more.

"Here we go," Arden muttered to himself. "Honestly, everything's fine, Gord. I just want to get some sleep."

Gord took a moment, eyeing the boy closely, but Arden remained confident and kept his composure. The Ogre huffed, then pivoted his body to the side, leaving his son just enough room to squeeze by into the house.

The following day, Arden, Gord, and Mugz ventured to Lake Stillwater, a secluded pond nestled deep within the woods.

Despite its modest size, the lake was always teeming with life. The trees swayed with the gentle breeze while scrawny sickle fish darted through the murky waters below.

Patches of lily pads crowded the shoreline, and the reeds danced with the tune of the wind.

For Arden, this lake was home to more than just thriving creatures and beautiful sights; it held cherished memories as well: the first time he caught a fish, the many days that Gord spent carving their rowboat, and their ongoing contest of "who could snatch the longest sickle fish."

Gord took charge as they arrived, fetching their boat amidst the trees and lifting it into the emerald waters. Mugz eagerly hopped aboard with a joyful chirp, and Arden climbed in after. With a hefty thud, Gord jumped into the boat then grabbed the oars from the floor and rowed out to the heart of the pond.

Once they'd found a sufficient spot, Arden gathered their two fishing rods crafted from gnarled branches and strong vines. This time, he claimed the longer pole for himself, purposely handing his father the shorter one instead.

Gord raised an unamused brow.

"Don't give me that look," Arden said. "You always get the good one, and you know it."

Gord humbly agreed with a shrug but quickly swiped the long rod from his son's grasp.

And someday, when you're worthy enough to use it, then you can have the good one, he signed with a smirk.

Arden rolled his eyes with a grin.

For a fleeting moment, the boy felt a sense of normalcy return. He was transported to simpler times when he was just a young child fishing with his father. The memories flooded back—the lazy afternoons by the water, the soothing sounds of nature, and the joy of spending time together without a care in the world.

The rest of their afternoon was spent fishing, but Arden

struggled to catch anything of substance. Even Mugz tried to snag some gloon fish herself, but the plump creatures were far too slippery for her little teeth. Gord, however, had a hearty pile of sickle fish going, as usual.

Arden grumbled, trying to stave off the jealousy coursing through his veins.

Just then, a massive creature latched onto the hook of his fishing rod and gave a powerful tug, pulling the boy upright. Arden braced himself, digging his feet into the boat's floor to reel. With all of his might, he wrestled against the unseen adversary, but as the struggle grew intense, he felt his arms ready to give out.

A chubby gloon fish, speckled with white spots, burst from the water, soaring briefly before plunging back toward the pond. Arden yanked the rod with all of his might, but the creature's weight was too much for him to handle. With a splash, the gloon slammed into the water, shattering the rod in two and drenching Arden in a thunderous wave.

"Well, I guess you win again, Gord," said the boy with disappointment.

Better luck next time, his father signed with a shrug.

Arden bent over the edge of the boat, twisting his drenched clothes to squeeze out the water. By the time the final drops fell from his cloak, the lake had grown still once more. He found himself gazing at the hazy reflection of his own eyes upon the water. His mind drifted, replaying the strange events of the previous night. A knot of unease tightened in his stomach, and with a heavy sigh, he slumped back onto the boat's bench, his face blank and weary.

Noticing his son's face, Gord snapped to get his attention.

It's about last night, isn't it? he signed.

Though unsure of how his father would react to such a peculiar tale, Arden nodded his head anyway. He just couldn't withhold such an eerie truth.

"When I sat on the stoop last night, a strange wind rushed past me. After it was gone, everything went still. No sounds, no breezes—nothing."

Gord shrugged, then signed, *These spring nights bring many rogue winds.*

"There's more," Arden continued. "I also noticed this blue fog that rolled in from the trees. It moved like... like tentacles—then it stopped and rose into a wall."

The boy's father rubbed his chin briefly, then replied, *Perhaps a trick of the moonlight?*

Arden sighed, struggling to express what he witnessed. "I thought the same thing at first, but then I saw something glowing behind the fog, like eyes watching me."

Gord tilted his head.

"They were completely white—almost like that of a corpse. I didn't know whether I should run inside or just stay put. But then, I heard whispering voices; a group of women, I think, or maybe just one. They told me to follow them—they claimed to know about my stone, too."

The stone? Gord asked, sitting straighter.

"Yes," Arden replied. "They said if I went with them, they would tell me its secrets, why I had it, and where it came from. They even called me... their son."

Gord's brow began to glisten. He reached his trembling hands upward to sign, *Did you believe them?*

Arden began to play with his nails.

"Well, not at first," he said, meekly looking away toward the shore. "I wanted to head back inside but felt like I was stuck to the stoop. The more the women spoke to me, the more I listened, but I had no control over it. Their voices got closer like they were right there in my head... reaching for my very soul."

A loud smash echoed through the air as Gord jolted into the boat's stern with terror. The sudden impact thrust Arden and Mugz backward, smacking their heads on the railing.

"Ow!" the boy yelled, his eyes locking onto Gord.

The Ogre frantically offloaded their entire catch of fish, then scrambled for the oars.

"What's wrong with you? We need those!" Arden exclaimed.

Gord disregarded his son's questions and Mugz's fearful barks, swiftly propelling them toward the shore with great strength. Muck and grime splashed about, soaking their rowboat with every paddle.

Arden pried for an explanation, though it was useless. Gord clearly had no intention of answering. Why was he so shaken? If his father *knew* something about this mysterious woman, then why was he keeping it a secret? Perhaps her claims of being the boy's family were true after all. A horrible thought crossed Arden's mind... What if Gord was purposely keeping him from his birth family?

CHAPTER 5
TROUBLE IN BANN-GAR

The boat hit the muddy shore with a loud thud. Gord leaped straight out, hurled the oars into the woods, and grabbed his son by the arm.

"I don't understand," Arden shouted as his father pulled him through the dense woods. "Tell me what's going on!"

Urgency sparked in Gord's eyes as he weaved through the trees. His erratic and unpredictable navigation left Arden battered by twigs and vines with every turn.

Mugz scampered close behind, whimpering as she followed the Ogre's chaotic trail.

After what felt like hours, the trio finally arrived at their home. Gord slammed the front door shut and pushed Arden deep into the room as Mugz ran to her nest to hide.

The Ogre collected everything within reach—books, cooking pots, chairs, and even the dining table. In a hurry, he shoved all of it toward the door, barricading them inside.

"Gord, stop!" Arden shouted, trailing his father around the house. "Why are you acting like this?"

Gord refrained, cutting the boy a sharp glance before rummaging once more. He tossed around piles of clothing and ransacked every cabinet. Then he took three burlap sacks and tossed in everything that was left: weapons, utensils, food. He was just about to grab the half-used candles when suddenly, a wooden bowl hit the back of his neck.

Gord turned around to find his son leering at him.

"What is it going to take for you to tell me what's happening?" the boy demanded. "A bigger bowl? A rock? Because I'll go get one."

Gord's heavy breathing eased as he took a moment to soothe his panic.

There's no time to explain. We must leave right now, he signed.

"No! I'm not going anywhere. You haven't told me a thing since we left the lake. If this has to do with my birth family, Gord, then I have a right to know!"

The Ogre dropped his bag to the floor.

Look, whatever those strangers, those things, told you last night was a lie. They're not Elves, and they're definitely not your family.

"How can you be so sure?" Arden snapped.

Gord huffed. He stomped over to the barricaded door and snatched a chair from the towering pile of junk. Placing it down to take a seat, he motioned for Arden to sit on his bed.

The young Elf growled under his breath but sat, waiting with arms crossed.

Son, what I'm about to explain, you must believe my every word, Gord signed, casting the boy a stern glance. *Those eyes you saw, I have seen them myself. They belong to a group of people you've never encountered. Until this very moment, I believed them all to be dead, but now I see that is far from true.*

The Ogre paused, shaking his head. *I never thought I'd have to bring up their name again.*

"Who are they?" Arden asked.

The Or'Ackins, Gord signed with a shiver. *Wicked beings*

unlike any other in Cynorrum. Their rotted, beaked faces still haunt me, as do the terrible things they've done—things I still can't fully understand.

Trying to wrap his head around his father's description, Arden asked, "Where have you seen them before?"

Gord glanced out the window as rain began to fall from the sky. His eyes flooded with the sorrow of long-repressed memories.

It was ages ago, on a night like this, he signed. *I was just a child, living amongst the Ogres in the mountain regions of Bann-Gar. My people were caring folk, unlike the monsters everyone had imagined us to be.*

For a moment, Gord's eyes glistened with happiness as he recalled his fellow Ogres, but it was short-lived.

"What happened?" the boy inquired.

A terrible wind swept through our village, just like the one you encountered last night, Gord signed. *At first, we Ogres thought it was just a storm approaching. But then, a mysterious fog crept in from the north, and the silhouettes of three Or'Ackins emerged. Not a blink came from their glowing white eyes as they strode atop their gringores: ugly creatures mightier than a bear. By the time we were able to get a good view of the Or'Ackins, it was already too late.*

"They attacked you?" Arden asked.

No, Gord signed. *But they spoke to us in the same way those women did to you last night. Not aloud, but in our minds: our very souls. They made us believe in thoughts that were not our own and tricked us into following them to Havarria: their homeland of eternal, blizzarding night. It was there that the Or'Ackins council of sorcerers practiced their illusions, their powers—*

"Whoa, wait a minute," Arden said, quickly stopping his

father. "Sorcerers? Powers? What do you mean?"

Gord signed even faster, his hands trembling. *I've seen some of the Or'Ackins turn people to stone, freeze them to ice, and corrupt their minds with a sinister practice known as soul-charming.*

Arden shook his head. Gord must have been exaggerating. It was decades ago, and the Ogre was just a child then. How could he have remembered the Or'Ackins so accurately? A kingdom of people with bird skull heads and a council of sorcerers? That couldn't possibly exist! Not even in a land as diverse as Cynorrum.

"Gord, are you saying that some of these beings are... magical?" Arden inquired. "I'm sorry, but that can't be true."

Son, the Ogre signed. *The Or'Ackin sorcerers—they're unlike anything you can imagine. They can invade the deepest part of your soul and convince you to do their evil bidding, even make you kill your closest friend if they wish.*

"I don't know if I can believe this," Arden said, standing up from his bed. "Look, if you're just trying to scare me into staying by your side at all times, forget it. I'm not a child anymore!"

Gord immediately sprung to his feet, knocking his stool to the floor. The loud thud echoed throughout the house. He took a step closer to the boy with a massive shadow that engulfed half the room.

Arden slumped back onto his bed, his confidence fading. Gord's expression was unlike anything he'd seen before. His usually calm and gentle features were contorted with fear and urgency, a look that made Arden feel as if he were face-to-face with a total stranger. He never knew Gord could be so terrified. The Ogre couldn't have been lying, not with a reaction like this.

Gord watched his son's stare turn into that of horror. Upon the realization, the Ogre slowly melted back into his former self. He picked up his chair and sat back down with a heavy sigh.

This was a time in my life I had hoped to forget, but it's all true, he signed calmly. The Or'Ackin sorcerers attempted to soul-charm many other beings throughout my younger years. And those who weren't easily bewitched were punished, lured away, and forced to drink a horrible potion.

Gord's eyes glistened. A tear trickled down his cheek

I can still remember its bitter taste. It poisoned my tongue and took my voice away forever.

Arden shuddered in fear as a bolt of lightning struck out in the woods. He had no idea Gord went through such a terrible experience, nor did he understand why his father couldn't speak, but now it all made sense. And to think he had previously believed all Ogres were mute.

"H-how did you get away from the Or'Ackins?" Arden stuttered as if affected by the potion himself.

Gord signed, *My mother and I weren't as easily controlled by their soul-charms. After our voices had been stolen, we developed our own sign language, in secret, and fled with a few mute Ogres in the night. We ran for days without look-ing back, eventually making our way to the forests of Graveen. We barely escaped with our lives.*

Gord hung his head in sorrow, letting out a sniffle.

Arden took a deep breath, his eyes growing sad for his father's past. He slowly stood up from his bed and placed a gentle hand on the man's shoulder.

Mugz hopped onto Gord's lap. He patted her on the head, then looked at his son once more.

Those voices you heard last night, I believe it was a single person, he signed. A powerful Or'Ackin sorceress who will likely stop at nothing to get your stone. Staying here would only put us in great danger.

Arden sat back down, nervously. "Where will we go? I've never left the southern woods before."

Gord thought for a moment, biting the nail of his thumb.

I know a safe place: one of my old homes from after I es-caped Havarria, he signed. It's about a day's journey north. We'll stay here tonight, but tomorrow we should leave at sun-rise.

"We don't have a choice in this, do we?" Arden asked, now feeling miserable at the thought of abandoning their lives in Noakwood Hollow.

Gord nodded regretfully.

The boy sighed. His feelings for the Or'Ackins were somewhere between terror and fascination. He questioned how anyone could have such mysterious abilities, but more importantly, why they sought his stone. What was it worth to them, and how far were they willing to go to retrieve it? None of this would've happened if he didn't have this stone in the first place.

Upon that realization, a thought crept into the boy's

mind, urging him to consider it. He turned back to his father with a spark in his eyes, eager to share this new idea.

"Gord! If we run now, we may be fleeing from this Or'Ackin forever. But what if I could get rid of the stone somehow?"

Gord tilted his head.

"Finn!" Arden said. "Think about it. He's a gemologist. If that Noamin knows anything, it's stones. Maybe *he* can remove it."

You want to go back to Mogoroth? Gord signed.

"I know it sounds insane, but it would only be for a little while," Arden said, trying to sway his father's judgment. "Just enough time for Finn to help me."

It's too risky, Gord signed. *You've never revealed this stone to anyone before, voluntarily, that is. Who knows what someone's intentions might be? Even Finn. He might want the stone for himself or have allied with that Tetran jeweler.*

"What? No. Finn would never turn on me like that, and he definitely wouldn't work with Big Fish. They've probably never met each other anyway."

You don't know for sure who Finn is associated with, Gord signed.

"Well, what else are we supposed to do?" Arden asked. "We can't run forever. If this works, then we might have a shot at getting this Or'Ackin off our backs."

Gord thought carefully about his son's plan, but eventually signed, *If I let you do this, you cannot be seen by anyone. Do you understand?*

Arden nodded.

We'll stop there tomorrow before we head north, Gord continued. *We should still have enough time to make it to my old home before dark. Now get some rest. You'll need it.*

CHAPTER 6

THE GEMOLOGIST

Arden awoke at dawn to see his father asleep in a chair by their window. The poor Ogre must've been up all night, scanning the woods for the Or'Ackin sorceress.

As the boy took his first step out of bed, Gord immediately sprung awake, snapping a paranoid glance in his direction.

"Just me," Arden said quickly.

The Ogre slouched back into his seat, waving a tired hand.

Did you rest well? he signed.

"As best I could," Arden replied. "What about you?"

Gord shook his head, then peered out the window. A layer of gray clouds still smothered the sky from the night before.

We should pack our things.

Arden gave a weak nod. He was dreading this moment. Leaving home forever was a terrifying thought, but he tried to kindle an ember of optimism anyway. He'd always been curious about the lands beyond Noakwood Hollow. Perhaps it was time to embrace that, even if it meant abandoning all he'd ever known.

With time pressing on, they collected whatever they could carry in their hands, bags, and paws. Gord gathered the essentials and an old wooden flute he'd kept from his youth. Mugz fetched the stash of muttleberries from her nest. Lastly, Arden packed his slingshot and a leather pouch containing five hundred chip—all that was left to their name.

Once their packing was finished, the trio walked outside and descended the hill, their footsteps echoing in the solemn quiet of Noakwood Hollow. In unison, they all turned to gaze at their home nestled amongst the towering trees.

Happy memories whispered around them like gentle breezes: meals shared around a crackling fire, games played in the yard, and sunsets watched as they sat on the cliffs of Noakwood Hollow.

Those moments felt so much brighter and full of innocence back then, a stark contrast to the somber reality they faced now. Today, it seemed everything was cloaked in a veil of gloom.

Merely a few weeks ago, Arden would've found it hard to imagine a life worse than his own: living in such a small home with barely anything to his name. But now, the boy felt guilty for that past sentiment. As much as he loathed that crammed little house, with its one room and rotting walls, it was still a sanctuary, a roof over his head. Even on its worst days, like in winter when the fireplace's warmth escaped through the cracks in the walls or in spring when rain found its way inside, this humble abode always felt welcoming and safe.

Standing there, looking back at their old cottage, Arden realized the weight of leaving it for good. It wasn't just about saying goodbye to the physical place; it meant leaving behind a piece of his childhood as well. The thought of venturing into the unknown was daunting, and he couldn't help but wonder if they were making the right decision. Yet, deep down, he knew there was no turning back.

Arden hung his head in sorrow.

"This is it," he said. "We can never return. We have no home anymore."

Gord knelt to meet Arden's eyes, his stare serious but loving.

Of course, we do, son, he signed. *We have each other. Home is not a house; it's the people you hold closest to your heart, the ones who will always stand by your side, no matter the distance. You will always be my son, Arden. My home.*

A tear swelled in Gord's eye as he motioned his last word close to his chest.

Arden leaned in, embracing his father tightly.

After the tender hold, they shouldered their bags and walked away without a backward glance.

Their journey to Mogoroth was plagued by an unsettling silence. They hadn't left Noakwood Hollow in nearly half a month, and up until a few days ago, there were no signs of danger knocking at their door. But now, with this Or'Ackin on their trail, even the snapping of a twig left Arden and his family on high alert. The sorceress could have been hiding anywhere, waiting for the proper moment to strike. The best Arden and his father could do was to keep moving and hope that they weren't leaving too many tracks.

When they finally reached the winding docks of the black market, Arden hesitated at the forest's edge. He hoped people had forgotten about his secret stone within the past twenty days, but that seemed unlikely. Arden just prayed that Finn had an answer to his problem, aside from hiding away forever.

"Is this even worth the risk?" Arden asked with doubt. "What if Finn can't be trusted like you said? What if I go in, and there's a trap waiting for me?"

Gord nodded slowly.

Arden reflected for a moment, then shook his head.

"I need to see if the stone can be removed. Otherwise, I'll regret never trying." The boy took a deep breath and shrugged off his fears, leaving them at the docks' edge. "Alright. Here goes nothing... or everything."

Determined, Arden pulled his hood over his head, snuck onto the pier, and rode down the Mogo-lift that would get him closest to Finn's shop. Thankfully, there were few ships or people outside to witness the Elf. At this hour, only those who traveled from a far distance would be awake to open their markets, and Finn was one of those people.

As Arden sifted through the crowd, he stuck to the

shadows, cautious not to draw any attention. Creeping through the market, he eventually reached his destination: an old familiar gem stand with its old familiar owner, standing atop a small stool.

To no surprise, Finn was consumed by a search for something amongst his pile of gems.

"Oh! Where is that thing?" the Noamin cried out, wiping the sweat above his giant teal goggles.

Arden crept behind the tent, surveying the frenzied man and his wild, jewel-scattered hair.

"Psst. Finn. Hey, Finn!" he whispered.

Still unaware of Arden's presence, the Noamin continued his frantic search.

Obviously, this guy wasn't going to notice the Elf anytime soon, and Arden couldn't afford to just sit and wait around. So, in a swift movement, he grabbed ahold of Finn's tattered scarf and yanked it straight down.

A gasp left the old man's fuzzy lips as he turned around and spotted the boy.

"A-Arden! What brings you here?" he whispered. "You shouldn't have come back. Big Fish has been looking everywhere for you. You could've been spotted!"

"I wasn't," Arden muttered quietly, joining Finn's side below the counter.

"Well, I sure hope so... for your sake," the Noamin said. "Big Fish says you're pawning off fake jewelry. I thought you knew better than that, lad."

Finn shook his head in disappointment, returning to his inventory.

"Hey, wait a minute," Arden said, tugging at the old man's leg. "I didn't know the necklace I traded was fake. If I had, I wouldn't have stolen it in the first place. But listen, I have to ask you something very important."

Finn paused. "Like what?"

"Have you overheard any other rumors about me?" Arden asked.

The old Noamin fiddled the ends of his beard, trying to recollect his thoughts.

"Well, come to think of it... yes," he said. "But what I've heard makes little sense." Finn scratched the back of his head unsurely, almost afraid to recite the strange rumor. "The folks around here are saying you've got a blue thingy in your chest or something. I don't know."

Arden's expression warped into a grave mess.

"Oh gracious, lad. It's true, isn't it?"

"That's why I came to see you—why I need your help," Arden said meekly.

"My help?" Finn asked. "How could I possibly help with something like *that*?"

"Well, because I think it's a stone," Arden said.

Finn hopped down to the ground from his stool, his wide ears waving in the air. "Interesting! Mind if I take a look?"

Arden nodded, his fingers trembling as he unfastened the top strings of his shirt. The thought of willingly exposing this secret to Finn made him uneasy. The boy hesitated for a moment, taking a deep breath before slowly revealing the stone embedded in his chest.

Finn's brow flew high.

"How peculiar," he said, more so to himself than to Arden.

"Can you tell me what it is?" the boy inquired, his voice tinged with anticipation and fear.

"Perhaps," Finn replied. "But I would have to examine it first. Just stay right here."

The old Noamin arose from the floor and began to rummage through his bags even more chaotically than before.

Arden waited, wondering what Finn could be searching for above the counter. He attempted to peek, but a shiny object flew right past his head and crashed to the floor.

"Hey!" the boy shouted in a whisper. "Watch it."

"Here it is!" Finn exclaimed.

The old man leaped down, holding what appeared to be some sort of telescope. The object was decorated with all kinds of sharp needles and odd, pointed gadgets.

"What's that?" Arden asked in a trembling voice as he stared at the device's long prongs.

"Don't worry, it shouldn't hurt a bit. This little gizmo *here* will help me get a better look at what you've got *there*."

The old man placed the device's monocle on his left goggle and leaned in close to the boy's torso, pressing the other end onto the stone.

Arden winced at the cold sting of the looking glass. The sensation was stranger than he could have imagined. He'd never had anything besides his own hands touch the stone.

"How long have you had this?" Finn asked, cranking a small handle on the side of his contraption.

Arden pondered for a minute.

"Since before I can even remember," he said. "Gord assumed I was born with it, but I'm not so sure."

The Noamin began to twist another knob, then mumbled, clearly not listening to the story.

"You know, I really appreciate this," Arden continued, watching the old Noamin conduct his work. "It's funny. I was almost worried that you'd turn me away and say—Ow!"

The device's needles began to jab at the stone rapidly. A shooting pain spread through Arden's chest, causing his back to tingle for a moment.

"Damn it!" he snapped. "You said it wasn't going to hurt!"

Finn backed away, bellowing a nervous chuckle as he removed the monocle from the boy's chest. "I lied. Sorry, lad."

Arden tied the strings on his shirt to prevent the Noamin from experimenting any further.

"So?" he asked.

Finn wiped his magnifier clean with the end of his scarf, then said, "From my observation, it is indeed a stone, and I'd say this thing was placed into your chest deliberately."

"Deliberately? You don't think I could've been born with this?"

"Judging by the scar tissue surrounding it... not likely."

"Do you have any idea why someone would do this to me then?"

"I have no idea, lad. *I didn't place it there.*"

Arden dropped his head in disappointment.

"I'm sorry," Finn continued, "but it's too old for my expertise."

Arden sat up straighter and peered down at the stone with a newfound curiosity.

"Really?" he asked. "How old do you think?"

"Hard to say. But my guess... very old, maybe even before our time," Finn replied, packing the monocle into his bag. "I mean, I've seen a lot of stones pass through Mogoroth, but nothing like what you've got there."

Arden mulled over this new information for a moment, then turned to his friend and asked, "Can it be removed?"

"Ha!" the Noamin cackled. "You're joking, right? Just a moment ago, I barely tapped it, and you jumped higher than a thistle leaper. Removing it could be dangerous... might even kill you. Why would you even think of such a thing?"

"Isn't it obvious?" Arden asked somberly. "Just look at all the trouble it's been causing me."

"Ah, yes. You've got a point there," Finn replied, itching the bumps on his nose. "I don't know about removing it here, but you could always try the... No, no! What am I thinking? It'd be too risky, especially for someone your age."

"What? What would be too risky?" Arden pressed.

Finn waved his hand. "It was a horrible idea. Just forget I said anything at all."

"But I don't have many options left, and if I don't get rid of this thing somehow, I'll be on the run forever! Please,

Finn, you've got to tell me."

"Oh, alright," the old man groaned. "There is a legend—one that dates back ages ago. A myth from a place so vile and so dark that even during the day, there is barely any sun to lighten its paths."

Finn's expression fell grim as if he'd just seen death itself. He lifted his goggles, revealing his beady black eyes, then whispered, "Have you ever heard of Blackwater Swamp?"

Arden pondered. "Maybe once before. I'm not really sure."

Finn stared at him intensely. "People say that place holds greater secrets than any other. Some believe it to be haunted, but I think it's more mystical than anything. No one knows why, but most who venture there rarely return, and if they do, they never come back the same."

"You're doing a pretty good job of creeping me out, Finn," Arden said. "But what does this swamp have anything to do with my stone?"

"Well... there's this *thing* that lives in Blackwater," Finn said ominously. "It's something old, something ancient. Its true name hasn't been spoken in so long that it's been lost to time. Some say this creature is as tall as a noakwood, with a twisted body and hair like vines. Others say that it's a being of pure disgust, with three eyes that can see futures yet to come. But no matter what, all the tales describe it as a deceptive monster that uses tricks to keep its victims there... forever."

Arden's heart quickened. The idea of such a creature's existence was hard to fathom. It almost seemed more horrifying than the Or'Ackins and their soul-charming.

"So what is this beast called?" he asked.

Finn rubbed his elbows for comfort as chills slipped down his spine, rattling his bony knees. "The Witch of Blackwater Swamp."

"Oh, you've got to be kidding me," Arden muttered, sinking his face into his hands. And just when he thought the stories about terrifying monsters had all but been spent, here comes Finn with another. How could his situation get any worse?

A haunted swamp inhabited by an evil witch. Great. Just great, he thought.

Finally, building up some courage to speak, Arden asked, "Well, do you think this witch can remove it? I mean, I can't go out to a place like that just for more information. I *need* this stone gone. Like, dropped into an ocean or something."

"I can't say for sure," Finn answered, his expression solemn. "Honestly, there may be no one else alive who *can* remove it. That witch is your best bet now. But heed my warning, lad, venturing into the swamp could change you, and not for the better. Truly, I'd advise against it."

Arden sighed. The idea of such a perilous quest was daunting, even for someone as desperate as he, but it still had to be considered.

"Finn, there are people that want this stone so much that they may even kill me for it. Don't you see? I have to get rid of this. It's not exactly a choice."

Finn hesitated. "If this is what you have to do, then I think I know a guy who might be able to guide you. He's a stubborn Leptoid who goes by the name Buffoh. As I recall, he used to lead travelers through the swamp—for a price, of course."

Arden leaned in close. "Where can I find him?"

Finn seized a piece of parchment from a cubby above the counter. "Anura village, just a day's travel north of here on foot." He pulled a long quill from his beard and began to draw a map. "Now, when you get there, look for a shop called "The Gribic's Eye." That's where you'll find Buffoh. If you pay him enough, he should help you. Oh, and that reminds me, when you meet him, be sure to tell him he still owes me fifty chip for spending the entire afternoon with that strange cousin of his."

"Alright," Arden said.

The old Noamin finished sketching the last few lines and handed the boy the wrinkled piece of paper.

"Now, get out of here, lad," Finn said, shoving his hands toward the boy hastily. "This place will be crawling with shoppers any moment."

Arden's heart swirled with a mixture of hope and uncertainty as he pocketed the map.

He gave a grateful nod, then raised his hood and said, "Thank you, Finn. I really appreciate it."

Chapter 7

AN OLD HOME

Arden raced back to his father as quickly as possible to share Finn's news of his stone, dodging glances in the bustling crowds.

When he finally reached the woods outside Mogoroth Bay, Gord was nowhere in sight.

"Gord? Mugz?" he whispered with urgency, removing his hood to get a better look.

From behind a nearby tree, his father and mugget companion cautiously peeked out.

How did it go? Gord signed, stepping into view.

Arden, still out of breath, replied, "Well, we've been right about one thing. What I bear is definitely a stone and apparently an ancient one."

Ancient?

Arden nodded. "Finn believes it was put in my chest on purpose, though he's not sure why."

That's strange, Gord signed. *Did he at least know how to get rid of it?*

"No, but he suggested another option. There may be someone else who can remove the stone without harming me. Although, getting to them may take a few days."

Arden hesitated. He knew that revealing this whole Blackwater Swamp plan would elicit a strong reaction from his father.

So, who is this mysterious person? Gord signed.

Arden's hands trembled, and his mouth went dry, but he mustered the courage to say the words as swiftly as he could, "The Witch of Blackwater Swamp."

Gord shook his head in discontent, then signed, *Absolutely not. There's no way we're going anywhere near that forsaken swamp, let alone a witch.*

"But what if this is the only way?" Arden pleaded.

Gord remained strict on the matter and signed, *It's far too dangerous. Believe me, son, nothing good can come from witches. Having met a few sorcerers myself, I can say that with confidence. Now, we need to do what's best for all of us: travel to my old home and stay safe.*

The Ogre reached for his son's arm, but Arden jolted back.

"By safe, you mean hide for the rest of my life?"

Gord's expression hardened. *I'm not saying we'll be there forever, but at least until this Or'Ackin leaves us alone. We tried the Finn idea and it didn't work out. So, if heading up north ensures our well-being, then we will do exactly that.*

Arden groaned. The weight of defeat pressed heavily upon him, but he couldn't deny that Gord's logic held merit. Despite his burning desire to dispose of the stone, Arden had to admit that embarking on a journey into the swamp was a perilous idea.

Come on, Gord signed. *There are some ships approaching the docks. It's best we leave now before more show up.*

Arden held his tongue and nodded bitterly.

They gathered their bags from the ground and left without another word.

As they disappeared into the wilderness, a massive ship with burgundy sails arrived at the shores of Mogoroth Bay.

Its immense flag billowed in the wind with a fierce symbol that resembled a white deer skull.

From the main deck, twenty Dacarri soldiers emerged, riding atop giant bull-pigs. Their menacing appearance was equally foreboding, as was their cruel leader: a proud man with large antlers and an ancient ax holstered to his back.

Lord Zark had finally come to claim the stone.

Arden and Gord had trekked the entire day without pausing once for food or water. As night began to fall, the Ogre's determination to reach his old home was amplified by a deep fear of what the darkness might bring. They both knew that the Or'Ackin sorceress would soon be on their trail, and no one in their right mind would risk lingering around.

Gord marched relentlessly, making it a struggle for Arden to match his pace. It wasn't until his father finally stopped that the boy had a chance to catch his breath.

"What's the holdup?" Arden asked, his voice straining. "I thought we weren't going to stop until we—"

Arden silenced himself as he realized they stood before an old entryway covered in dead vines and dirt.

They had reached the Ogre village at last, or what remained of it.

Many of the rocky homes that filled its ruins were crumbling; their porches swallowed by moss and chimneys broken to pieces. Not a single plume of smoke billowed from their flues. Not one of their windows gleamed. It was clear that no one had been there in years.

"Gord, where is everyone?" Arden asked with concern.

The Ogre stood eerily still, his gaze fixed on the desolation before them. He began to walk through the abandoned village, lost in thought as his son and Mugz followed in his cautious footsteps.

Arden scanned the buildings for signs of life, but there were none. Torn articles of clothing had been scattered across the dirt. Cracked tools and bowls sat half-buried in the ground. The remnants of a campfire lay in a cold pile of ash.

"I'm sorry, Gord," Arden remarked. "I don't think this place is suitable for living in. I mean, look at these homes. They're falling apart."

The boy turned to his father, but Gord had walked to an overgrown garden in the distance. Dozens of triangular statues surrounded the clearing in a circular pattern. Gord stood motionless at the center, his back turned.

Arden approached him slowly, but the Ogre sank to his knees and buried his face in his palms.

Curious, Arden studied the surroundings more closely, realizing it wasn't a garden at all, but a graveyard. Resting atop the dirt sat twenty headstones; some sinking, others toppled from ages past. Illegible words and symbols had been inscribed on their cracked surfaces: the names of Ogres long departed.

"Is this why you left?" Arden inquired softly. "You were the last one?"

Gord lifted his head from his hands and rose to face his son, his lips quivering.

The Ogres I escaped with weren't as fortunate as I was, he signed shakily. *Many grew too old and sick to form families of their own. Over time, they faded away each year until*

Gord paused, his tears flowing like gentle streams. He glanced at the narrow gravestone behind him: his mother's resting place.

The nights became so lonely. There was no one to talk to or even shed tears with. Eventually, the weight of this place became too much to bear. So I took the little that I had left and journeyed south. I spent weeks searching for a new home, but everywhere I went, I was rejected, seen as a monster.

Finally, I turned to the Elves, but they too wanted nothing to do with me. I decided to live on the outskirts of Aramore instead, alone in an abandoned cave by a river with barely any fish. Given my meals were so scarce, I began stealing food from the Elves in the middle of the night just to survive.

Arden stood there in absolute astonishment. Now, he

understood the weight of his father's experiences. Gord's hardships surpassed anything the boy had ever endured.

As time passed by, I felt like there was no reason to go on until the day I found you abandoned by that river. The day you changed my life. If I hadn't kept you, I don't know what my purpose would've been.

Arden reflected on his father's laments. He respected the bravery it took for Gord to return to this village, especially knowing what buried sorrows the grounds held.

"Gord, I'm sorry. I can't imagine what you're feeling," Arden said gently. "And this place… there's so much pain here. I know it may be safer, but with the memories this village brings—you shouldn't have to relive it. I don't want you to."

His father stared at the grave in silence.

Arden continued with caution, "I know you don't think it's a good idea, but I still believe finding the witch in Blackwater Swamp is worth a shot. I mean, it definitely sounds crazy, but if I can get rid of this stone, then you won't have to—"

Gord turned to him swiftly and signed, *Please, son, I can't think about this right now. The thought of losing you is too much to bear, and I just won't risk it. I'm sorry, but I can't let you go there.*

Arden looked away in disappointment, but he understood his father's decision and didn't press any further.

Gord wiped the tears from his face and continued, *We're losing sunlight. We should start setting up a camp.*

For the remainder of that evening, they barely spoke, aside from figuring out what materials they would need to build a shelter. They gathered what they could and reinforced the least deteriorated structure in the village.

As Gord and Mugz drifted off to sleep, Arden stayed awake, as usual. The boy kept replaying the past couple of weeks in his head. He couldn't help but feel incredible guilt for his father and all that he'd put the man through recently. And now, this: reduced to hiding away in some crumbling old building.

Arden knew he was responsible for all of it, and the worst part was that he put his family in danger. He realized he was *still* putting them in danger. There was no telling what might come if someone had found them, especially that Or'Ackin. Hiding there—waiting for a seemingly unavoidable doom—it just didn't make sense.

Arden watched Gord and Mugz as they slept. Why should he continue to put them at risk? He needed to fix this once and for all. Alone. A difficult but necessary conclusion reached him: he had to leave tonight.

With that, the boy carefully arose from his place on the floor. He crept over to his satchel and picked it up quietly so as not to wake his father. Then he reached inside and slid out the map to Anura village that Finn had given him. Arden ripped off a section of the page that was left unmarked and scoured for something to write with.

On the ground beside him were a few charred pieces of wood from the fire they'd made. He picked one up, rolled it in the damp dirt, then pressed it to the torn parchment and wrote:

I'm sorry for everything. I've made too many mistakes and put you and Mugz in harm's way. I know you think we're safe here, but as long as I'm around, we'll never be. I'm going to find a way to get rid of this stone, for the sake of us all. Please don't come looking for me. I'll be back soon.

—Arden

CHAPTER 8

CLAW AND HOOK

Arden trekked into the woods, clutching Finn's map tightly. He had been wandering through the eve for a few hours now, and it seemed as though the further he went, the darker the woods became.

It was nearly pitch black outside, but the boy attempted to decipher the many symbols and directions on the old parchment. Squinting through the gloom, he surmised his location.

"Alright," Arden said to himself, comparing the forest to his map. "If the Ogre village is back west, then I must go..."

He could hardly make out the directions on the page but took his best guess.

"Northeast," he determined.

As he traveled, the trees in the surrounding area had abandoned their previously gnarled forms and began to adopt a more pole-like appearance. It was unlike any forest Arden had been through since the trees of Noakwood Hollow towered into the sky with their many twisting branches.

As he peeked up and examined the woods with curiosity, a splash of water landed directly on his head.

Arden held his gaze to the sky in surprise. Another drop fell into his eye and was followed by a thunderous boom.

"No," Arden whispered. He looked down at the map as its ink began to bleed and pool.

"Not now," he said in a panic. "I'm not even halfway there!"

A torrential rain poured violently, soaking the boy in moments. Scrambling to save the map from growing soggy, he stowed it back into his satchel.

Arden realized he had to stop until this storm passed. With a sigh, he trudged through the mud, his shoes sinking into the wet ground with every step.

Observing the area, he spotted a tree with a large enough canopy of leaves to keep him shielded from the downpour. Beside its trunk lay a fallen log that appeared dry enough to offer some shelter.

Grateful, Arden sat down, pressing his back against the timber's rough bark. He raised the hood of his cloak, further protecting himself from the elements.

The longer he waited, the more his boredom intensified. Arden sought any form of distraction. His fingers reached into his satchel, feeling the various contents until they closed around the familiar handle of his slingshot. He pulled it out, then picked up a few small pebbles from the ground. One by one, he launched them into the woods, listening as they disappeared into the shadows, counting each bounce. But with every shot, the boy's eyes grew heavier, and before he knew it, he had drifted off to sleep.

A few loud thuds echoed further off, snapping Arden out of his slumber. He bolted upright, unsure of how long he'd been resting.

The forest was eerily quiet.

Arden rubbed his eyes and glanced about, trying to identify the source of the thuds, but there was nothing in sight.

The rain must've stopped a while ago since the ground below his feet was no longer muddied, just damp. From the little he could see in the darkness, a pale fog now seemed to engulf the entire forest.

Suddenly, another set of thuds resonated through the mist, like the footsteps of an Ogre.

Arden shuffled a bit as he scanned the woods but was still unable to decipher which direction the sounds had come from.

"Gord?" he asked aloud, his voice trembling.

The stomping ceased, leaving the woods in silence yet again. Arden paused, but his breath quickened. With caution, he stretched his head upward to check behind the log, hoping to spot his father through the mist.

"Gord, is that you?" he repeated, his voice barely above a whisper.

A thunderous roar erupted from behind the fallen tree.

Arden gasped as a massive gringore lunged straight for him. The creature's long snout opened wide, revealing rows of sharp, rotted teeth.

Barely evading the beast's deadly bite, Arden threw himself to the side and darted into the thick fog. His whole body went numb except for his legs, which now seemed to be running on their own.

The creature's chaotic stomps and howls appeared to come from every direction, closing in on him with haste. Arden rushed ahead, casting worried glances over his shoulder.

Out of the darkness, a whooshing sound cut through the air and rushed toward the back of his neck. Arden turned to look, but his foot wedged beneath a root, sending the boy plummeting to the ground. He glared up in a panic as a boiling hot boomerang made of metal and bone emerged from the smog.

The fiery object hurled above, barely missing the boy's face. Like a knife through wax, the weapon scorched a tree up ahead, then quickly spiraled back from whence it came.

Arden twisted around to gain a better view as the blazing weapon flew back into the hands of a shadowy figure mounted atop the vile gringore. He squinted, trying to make out their features, but saw only a pair of piercing white eyes staring back at him.

Arden's stomach sank.

It was the Or'Ackin sorceress.

In a blink, the woman readied another throw and sent her boomerang zooming toward him.

Horror and shock surged as the boy braced for the impact: for his doom.

Just as the blade was about to strike Arden's head, a bronze hook swung out in front of him and deflected the boomerang. A brilliant flash and deafening clang burst out, rendering the boy temporarily blinded.

As his vision slowly returned, Arden found himself staring at the back of another mysterious figure: a hooded stranger with a hook for a hand. He noted the person's gray cloak and sand-covered shoes. Was this some sort of scavenger from the desert lands? Whoever they were, they paid little attention to Arden himself as they drew their focus to the Or'Ackin sorceress and her gringore.

Arden scampered to his feet, his limbs shaking as if they'd been frozen for hours. He took cover behind the nearest tree to hide, but it only provoked the gringore into a furious charge.

With a swift motion, the hooked stranger pulled a prickly object from their cloak and snapped it in their hand. In an instant, the coral-like item ignited into a violent frenzy of sparks.

Arden watched in awe as bright red embers went flying outward, sizzling loudly like meat over a fire. They radiated harshly, burning the gringore's furred body and illuminating the dark huntress atop it.

For a brief moment, the boy caught a glimpse of the Or'Ackin's terrifying face: a bird-skull head crowned with five bark points. She was even more terrifying than Gord had described.

Arden couldn't dwell there any longer. His instincts screamed for him to run, and he obeyed without hesitation. Refusing to look back for even a moment, the boy fled the duel. His heart hammered against his ribs, the sound of each beat thudding in his ears as he tore through the dense forest. Every step took him further from the gringore's painful screeches, which eventually faded to a distant echo. The pale fog began to dissipate under the moonlight and, with it, the bitter odor of that strange burning coral.

The whole scene thinned within Arden's mind, like the passing of a bad dream. He stopped and held his thighs, panting for breath until his thumping heart returned to a softer drum. Though the forest appeared much less menacing here, the boy knew he couldn't afford to stop just yet. He had to find a safer place to rest.

Inspecting the woods, Arden noticed a hollow space beneath a pile of boulders. It was large enough to fit in but just small enough for him to remain unseen.

He limped to the opening and crawled inside. It wasn't an inviting nook, nor was it cozy, and there were definitely bugs in there... but it *was* a place to sleep—much safer than being near those hunters, anyway.

Arden curled up into himself and attempted to rest through the remainder of the night, but the air grew frigid. On top of that, the ground here was still soaked from the storm before, making the dirt beneath his cloak feel much colder.

These discomforts, however, paled in comparison to the chilling reality that an Or'Ackin sorceress was indeed seeking him out after all. Having seen this dangerous woman in the flesh, the question irked him once more. Why would the Or'Ackins want his stone so badly that they'd kill him for it? And now there was this hook-handed scavenger to worry about, too. The fears piled in Arden's mind, adding to the ones already there.

As dawn approached that next day, the boy awoke from his dreadful slumber. He had barely slept five full hours, and his body ached from lying on the rocky ground. Groaning, he pushed himself up, eager to escape the unforgiving pit.

The morning mist clung to the air, veiling any sun that tried to break its dense barrier.

Arden surveyed his surroundings. There were no Or'Ackins. No gringores. No hooded figures in sight. At last, he was alone once again in a woodland he knew nothing about. How far he had traveled was completely uncertain.

But one thing was clear: he was nowhere close to Anura village.

Remembering Finn's map was tucked safely in his bag, Arden retrieved it and studied the parchment once more. The ink had been smudged in several places, obscuring some markings, but he could still discern enough to correct his course. It seemed he'd gone too far east now. So, with a heavy sigh, he began to trek westward, set on reaching his destination.

As the morning carried on, Arden stumbled across a cluster of odd-looking trees. Curved and blackened scorch marks were dug into their bark skin, still left smoldering, as if previously set ablaze. They must have been struck by the Or'Ackin sorceress's boomerang. Arden's pace quickened as he realized he was nearing the battleground from the night before.

Going deeper, the boy's cautious steps brought him to a familiar tree: the one he hid behind when the hook-handed stranger had arrived. At its roots were the dying embers of something still flickering. It appeared to be a burgundy chunk of bark, smoke bleeding from one of its edges.

Arden grabbed the peculiar fragment carefully, bringing it closer to his gaze. The texture was grainy and splintered. A few wisps of ash gathered under his nose, stinging the inside of his nostrils. Arden winced at the sensation but inspected the bark further. Inclined to remove its smoldering ashes, he flicked the edges of the item, and a few sparks burst forth.

Quickly holding the mysterious thing away from his face, Arden realized this was no ordinary piece of bark; it was the coral-like object that the hooded scavenger had used the night before.

Perhaps this could come in handy, Arden thought. If it could scare off a gringore, who knows what else it could do? Even so, leaving it in the woods would be a foolish idea.

The boy gave it a quick blow to simmer its dying sparks, then gently placed it into his satchel with care.

With some glint of hope, he continued until he came upon a long dirt road that cleaved the forest in two. The path was straight and wide, without a single twist or turn. Though Arden couldn't see its end on either side, he was relieved to be on even ground. Taking one last glance at Finn's map, the boy noticed this road led directly to Anura. He couldn't have been more than an hour or two from finding his guide to the swamp.

Arden's hunger for answers propelled him forward, each step bringing him closer to the end of the path.

Finally, he spotted his destination. Up ahead was a towering wooden archway adorned with intricate carvings reminiscent of insects. Splashes of mud had been caked onto the bottom of its posts, and a large wooden fence spread out widely from either side. Upon the gate's entryway sat a large plaque that read, "Anura Village."

CHAPTER 9

THE GRIBIC'S EYE

Anura's only road was a chaotic scene as hundreds of toad people called Leptoids bustled about with glee. They scurried in all directions along the street—up, down, side to side—even lined the rooftops and porches.

Arden had never seen so many Leptoids in one place, not even at Mogoroth. It seemed that the townsfolk were preparing for a celebration of some sort. The boy noticed dozens of colorful banners all around the village with big golden letters that said, "The Festival of the Flies."

Children strung up paper lanterns adorned with intricate insect designs above each weathered porch, casting a soft, inviting glow. Others bustled about, arranging buffet tables draped with runners that mimicked delicate spiderwebs. Elders carefully placed glass jars on their doorsteps, each holding a single large omen fly. Arden assumed it must have been for some kind of contest, maybe to determine who had caught the biggest one.

The boy shrugged, his curiosity about the festival's preparations fading quickly. He had his own mission to focus on: locating Buffoh and braving the dreaded swamp—though he clung to the hope that his soon-to-be guide might dispel the grim rumors. Maybe the swamp wasn't as treacherous as everyone claimed. Perhaps Finn and Gord had simply exaggerated the dangers.

Throwing on his hood, Arden discretely ventured through the village.

"Alright," he whispered to himself. "The Gribic's Eye has got to be around here somewhere."

The boy scanned the identical wooden buildings, but not a single one had a sign or number to signify whether it was a shop, house, or even a restroom. The only real difference between the structures was their doors, but even those were all similar shades of green.

Continuing along the street, Arden grumbled in frustration as he realized he was approaching its end. Just as the boy was about to double back through the village, the last building came into view. Its appearance resembled every other establishment, but there was one key difference: a plaque hanging above the porch with a large reptilian eye painted upon it... a gribic's eye! It had been watching him from a distance all along.

The boy could hardly contain his excitement. He crossed the road and hurried up the creaky steps of the stoop, but a sudden wave of nervousness settled over him.

What if Buffoh refused to help him? Arden swallowed, steadying himself. With a quick breath, he opened the door, pushing the doubt aside.

As he entered, a small bell rang throughout the gloom of the store. Not a person or creature was in sight, only some dust bunnies hiding in the corners of the room.

"Hello? Is someone named Buffoh here?" Arden asked, his voice echoing through the stillness.

The room, though void of life, was cluttered with hundreds of unique objects. The Gribic's Eye appeared to be a pawn shop, but it certainly wasn't a charming one. Practically everything was old and rotting, even down to the nails in the floorboards.

Knickknacks and half-melted candles cluttered the shelves, while books and half-drunk wine bottles adorned the countertops and cabinets. Sprawled out across the ground was a mishmash of items ranging from grimy pots and pans to broken crates filled with torn blankets.

It was useless junk, all of it, but the most astonishing part was the outrageous pricing. Thirty chip for a rusted locket? Fifty for a broken compass? A hundred for a smelly boot?!

"No wonder there aren't any customers here," Arden muttered under his breath.

Nothing in that shop appealed to his eye—except a green shimmer glinting from a dark shelf. Curious to see what shiny object might be resting there, Arden walked over slowly. To his surprise, it wasn't a cracking pot nor a disgusting shoe, but an emerald chalice with a gold-plated rim.

Desire surged within the boy, that is, until he noticed the paper tag hanging from its braided stem. Two thousand chip?! How could anyone possibly afford that? And yet, the longing to own this exquisite cup remained strong. Arden wanted it. He *really* wanted it.

In a swift motion, he peered around the shop, seized the chalice, and brought it to the opening of his satchel.

"Ay!" croaked a voice from the back of the room.

Arden froze, nearly losing grip of the cup in his hand.

"That's two thousand chip ya know?" the voice barked.

Arden faced the counter along the back wall to find a short and top-heavy Leptoid standing beside it. Dressed in a brown vest and ragged green pants, the old man appeared as shabby as the items on display. Mismatched socks peeked above his tiny shoes, adding to his eccentric appearance.

"Oh, I was only looking at it," Arden said with a little chuckle as he shakily placed the chalice back onto the shelf.

The toad man squinted at him, tapping his long, thick fingers on the desk with a steady growl.

"Sure ya were," he said, moving behind the counter. "I bet it woulda looked real nice inside ya bag, too."

Arden went flush. "No, I wasn't trying to—"

"Are ya gonna buy somethin' or not?" the man snapped impatiently.

"No," Arden replied, attempting to appear less suspicious. "Actually, I'm here for something else. To see a guy named Buffoh... Is that you?"

The old Leptoid leered at Arden with his piercing orange eyes, then hopped onto a barstool behind the counter.

"No," he said, crossing his arms above his bulging stomach. "And what do ya need with him?"

Arden proceeded cautiously. "Well, a Noamin friend of

mine—Finn—told me I could find him here. He mentioned Buffoh might be able to do me a favor."

The man gave a guttural chuckle before returning to his icy stare. "Favor? I hate to break it to ya, but Buffoh ain't doin' *you* or anybody no favors."

Now, Arden was curious. "Well, how would you know that if I haven't even spoken with him yet?"

"I would know 'cause he's dead!" replied the old toad, quickly lifting a shrunken Haggart head from beneath the counter. "This is all that's left of him."

Arden gasped at the repulsive sight.

"Yeah," the man said in a satisfied whisper.

Arden knew something was amiss. This guy just *had* to be Buffoh. Finn said his guide would be a stubborn Leptoid, not a Haggart. Clearly, this man was lying about something.

Enticed to reveal the truth, Arden smirked and said, "Well, that's very unfortunate. I had quite an offer to make him—a rather enormous sum of money."

The young Elf teasingly pulled out a pouch from his satchel and held it out by its string. He shook the bag just enough to get a jingle from the chip inside.

Suddenly, the grumpy man's eyes widened like giant globes.

"Really? How much we talkin'?" he asked.

Arden retracted the pouch, reached in with a sifting finger, and said, "Well, I have five hundred chip. But minus the hundred that Buffoh already owes Finn—"

"Whoa," the old Leptoid interjected, leaning in closer. "A hundred chip? I... *Buffoh* said he only owed Finn fifty chip, as I recall."

"Oh. No," Arden replied calmly. "You must be mistaken. Finn specifically said that Buffoh owes him one hundred chip for spending a whole day with his strange cousin.”

The thin hairs on the man's head flew toward the ceiling. His eyes boiled as he threw the Haggart head down and jumped up onto the countertop.

“Ay! Watch it, kid,” he shouted, waving a chubby green finger near the boy's nose. “Don't call my cousin strange. Only I can do that.”

“Ah-ha!” Arden exclaimed, pointing a finger back at the Leptoid. “So, you *are* Buffoh, then.”

The man's shoulders sagged.

“Damn it,” he croaked under his breath, retreating below the counter.

A triumphant smile spread across Arden's face.

“Well, it's nice to finally meet you, *Buffoh*,” he declared confidently. “But why hide your identity? What's the big secret?”

Buffoh rolled his eyes, moving out from behind the counter with a beaten-up broom.

“There ain't no big secret, pal,” he replied, sweeping the dirt-caked floor. “Ya just can't be too careful these days. But now that ya know *my* name, who are *you*?”

The man's broom kicked up more dust than it removed, causing Arden to cough.

“I-I'm Arden,” the boy said, hacking.

Buffoh tossed the broom aside and snatched a feather duster with a single quill remaining on its handle.

“So what's this offer?” he asked, somewhat interested as he began wiping the shelves.

Arden cleared his throat. “Well, Finn said you used to guide people through the northern woods, and he mentioned you might take me through Blackwater Swamp if I paid you enough.”

Buffoh dropped his duster.

"Blackwater what?!" he shouted. "No, no, no. I don't do that trip anymore. You'll have to find yaself another guide."

Arden's voice quickened. "Find another guide? But I can't. You're my only hope right now. Finn promised me you would—"

Buffoh scurried over to him, hands trembling.

"Alright! That's it! I'm closin' up shop," he said, beginning to push the boy toward the open door. "Come on, kid. Ya gotta go."

Now being shoved toward the porch, Arden braced himself on the threshold. "Wait! What about the money I offered you?"

Buffoh slammed his face into Arden's back, using his forehead to push the boy out with more force.

"Uh-uh. No way!" he shouted. "No amount of money is gettin' me back in that swamp."

"But I really need—"

"For the last time," the man shouted, "I said—"

Suddenly, Arden's grip gave way, and he tumbled outside, taking the old Leptoid with him. They sprawled in opposite directions onto the porch, and the contents of Arden's satchel were flung across the stoop.

"I'm too old for that crap," Buffoh snapped, brushing off his clothes as he got back on his feet. "There's no way ya gettin' me in that place again—"

The Leptoid's words trailed off as something caught the corner of his eye. He spotted a single item peeking out from inside the boy's satchel.

"Ooh! What's this?" he asked, picking up the object.

It was the chunk of bark Arden had kept from the woods, still in perfect shape.

"You mean that thing?" the boy asked as he stood up, rubbing his sore elbow.

"This *thing*?" Buffoh mocked. "Do ya have any idea how rare spark bark is around here? Ya can only find this stuff in the deserts of Jenoha—and even there, it's pretty scarce. Sheesh, kid, this *thing* is more valuable than a bag of verdite chip."

"Huh. Spark bark?" Arden repeated. "That makes sense, I suppose."

Buffoh seemed engrossed by its appearance. Arden, noticing the man's glistening eyes and twitching fingers, snatched the bark right back and held it just out of reach.

"Ay!" Buffoh shouted.

"Take me through the swamp, and it's yours," Arden proposed swiftly, realizing he had the upper hand.

Buffoh leered at the boy with suspicion, scratching his hairy chest before bellowing a foul burp.

"Plus, two hundred chip," he demanded.

Arden gave a stern nod. "Deal."

Buffoh held out his hand for a confirming shake, and Arden gladly accepted, passing over the spark bark and chip. Afterward, he collected his scattered belongings from the stoop.

"Alright, alright," Buffoh whispered as the boy finished. "Let's just get inside—I don't want anyone seein' us out here."

Now, instead of pushing Arden *out* of the shop, Buffoh was shoving him right back *in*. Once they were both inside, the Leptoid shut the door, locked all three bolts, and walked off to the back of the room.

"So why are ya headin' to Mukkis anyway?" he called out,

disappearing into the depths of a closet behind the counter.

Arden reflected on the past few minutes. Convincing the man to take him had been difficult enough—mentioning that he was searching for a witch just seemed unwise.

"Mukkis?" he asked, changing the subject.

A growl of frustration trembled from the obscured closet.

"Yikes, kid," Buffoh said, peeking his head out into the doorway. "I thought ya'd at least know about Mukkis if ya goin' there. It's the name of the marshlands where Black-water Swamp resides."

"Oh, right," Arden replied, trying to act knowledgeable. "I knew that."

Buffoh's head tilted down, and his brow steepened.

"Sure ya did," he said before popping back into the closet. "So, what kinda weapons ya got in that bag ya carryin'?"

Amidst the start of Buffoh's unseen rummaging, Arden shouted back, "A couple of knives and a slingshot!"

The obnoxious noises stopped. Buffoh swiftly emerged, shaking his head and holding a bunch of random junk.

"Seriously? That's it?" he asked. "Those won't do ya any good out in the swamp. Here, take this sword and shield instead. They'll defend ya from the whistle-jack horn flies— nasty things they are. Stung me right on the rump once. What a terrible week that was."

Arden received what appeared to be two weapons: one made of ceramic and the other of bronze.

"Oh! Wow. Thank you!" he said. "This is just what I—"

The boy ceased his words.

It wasn't a sword or shield at all, but a single half of a giant rusty scissor and the lid of a cooking pot.

"Uh—these aren't weapons," he said, puzzled.

"What are ya talkin' about?" Buffoh asked with a judging look. "Of course they are. Look at this sword. It's longer than ya thigh."

Arden glanced at the man with confusion. "Then what about this lid? You know it goes to a cooking pot, right?"

Buffoh snatched the cover from the boy's grip, examining it from every angle.

"Hmm," he said with wonder. "Nah, ya just teasin' me, kid."

He tossed the lid back to Arden and removed a satchel from the hook on the closet door.

"There's some armor in this bag too," the man said, throwing it to the boy's feet. "Ya know, to keep ya safe from the standard stuff: spiddle roots, crogs... all that."

Now, even more perplexed, Arden shook his head.

Spiddle roots? Crogs? What was this guy even talking about? the boy wondered to himself. He realized how little he knew of the journey ahead.

"Is the swamp really as terrifying as everyone says it is?" he asked. "Finn told me people who enter it sometimes get lost... forever."

Buffoh let out a sarcastic chuckle. "More than just sometimes, kid, and believe me, that place has got a mind of its own. It can sense ya fears—feed off 'em and make ya see things that aren't real."

"Oh," Arden said, his nerves twitching. "So, how did *you* make it out alive all those times?"

Buffoh retrieved a stained and worn scroll from behind the counter.

"Because I always bring my trusty map—Oh, and one of *these* with me!" he said, grabbing another object from his vest pocket and tossing it to the boy.

Arden observed it. The item seemed to be a dust-covered ball of sorts, nearly the size of his fist.

"That's to bring ya luck," Buffoh said with a wide grin.

Arden turned the sphere over, glancing at the narrow pupil staring back at him. It was a hardened, reptilian eye!

Startled, Arden dropped it immediately, and Buffoh plunged to the floorboards, barely catching it in time.

"Careful, kid! Do ya know what would happen if ya dropped a gribic's eye?" he asked in a hurry. "Ya'd have runny bowels for a month! I'm not kiddin'. Happened to me about three times last year."

Arden squinted at Buffoh, unsure if the Leptoid was serious

Buffoh huffed, shoving the eye into Arden's satchel. "Trust me, without this thing, I wouldn't have made it outta the swamp. Just be glad I'm lendin' it to ya."

Grabbing the spark bark and his scroll, Buffoh continued, "Anyway, with my map, this spark bark, and the gribic's eye, you should have all the luck ya need."

Arden shrugged, feeling less confident in the man's guiding abilities.

"I hope you're right," he muttered.

"We'll be fine, kid," Buffoh reassured. "Now we've got a long trip ahead of us, so we'd better get some rest. You can stay in the guest room upstairs. Unless ya'd rather sleep down here."

Arden glanced around the cramped shop, but there wasn't a single place for him to sleep... comfortably, anyway.

"Upstairs is fine."

87

CHAPTER 10

HEADING TO BLACKWATER

The following day, there was a loud knock at the door of The Gribic's Eye.

Arden bolted up from the warm comforts of Buffoh's guest bed, fearing someone had come looking for him. He quietly snuck to the window for a peek, but with the years of dirt caked over the glass, it was of no use.

A muffled and kind voice called from outside, "Buffoh! Buffoh, are you in there?"

Arden sighed in relief. This certainly wasn't any of the hunters on his trail. He wiped the sweat from his forehead. It seemed the last few sleepless nights had gotten to him. He was nearly accustomed to waking up in danger at this point.

Another knock thudded at the door. Clearly, Buffoh hadn't noticed he had a visitor.

Feeling somewhat obligated to take part, Arden threw on his cloak, stepped out into the hallway, and tapped on Buffoh's door.

"Hey, someone's outside calling for you," the boy said.

There was no answer, not the creaking of a bed frame nor the shuffling of sheets.

Arden knocked harder. "Buffoh!"

The door swung open violently, revealing a red-eyed and very irate Leptoid.

Arden jumped back.

"Have ya ever heard of manners, kid?" Buffoh snapped, his glare beaming. "Don't ya know that people don't wanna be disturbed when they're sleepin'?"

"Sorry," Arden said. "I think a customer is waiting for you outside."

The voice called again, prompting Buffoh to see who it was. He wobbled downstairs as angrily as he could, then opened the front door.

Arden crept down the first flight of stairs, arching his head to catch a glimpse of the interaction from the shadows.

"Oh, hey, Lonny!" Buffoh exclaimed, suppressing his grumpiness. "How's it goin'?"

Lonny greeted Buffoh with glee as they walked to the back counter.

From what Arden could see, Lonny was a rather plump Leptoid but donned much cleaner clothes than Buffoh did, and socks that actually matched, too.

"How's that thing on ya sister's foot doin'?" Buffoh asked.

"Oh, much better since you gave me that soot mud to let her try," Lonny replied.

"Yeah? I'm guessin' that's why ya here again—to get another jar or somethin'?"

"No," Lonny answered. "I just wanted to see if you're making that omen fly cake for the festival again. The whole village has been talking about it."

Still hidden in the dark, Arden noticed Buffoh shake his head with disappointment.

"Nah. Sorry, Lonny. I can't this year. I'm not gonna be able to make the festival either—busy takin' some Elf kid up north for a few days."

Intrigued, Arden leaned in further, hoping the Leptoid wouldn't reveal much more of their business. It was in the boy's best interest to stay unknown.

"But it's the Festival of the Flies, Buffoh," Lonny said with shock in their voice. "You can't miss *that*."

Buffoh sighed.

"I mean, the kid wants me to take him to Blackwater Swamp—I don't know," the old man said, his expression souring. "He's payin' me good, at least."

"Oh, my! Blackwater Swamp?!" Lonny asked with a shiver. "Do you think you'll be alright?"

Buffoh waved off the worry. "Ah, we'll be fine. I've been there a few times before. Anyway, me and the kid have to get goin'. Gonna be a long trip."

Arden watched the old Leptoid shuffle around the counter, politely nudging his guest to the door.

"Oh, sure, sure!" Lonny said, walking to the front porch. "You go ahead. I'll see you soon, Buffoh. Take care of yourself, now."

After bidding the neighbor farewell, Buffoh's sweet attitude quickly warped back to bitterness. He spun directly toward Arden, seemingly aware the boy was hiding in the stairwell all along.

"Well, don't just stand there, kid. Get over here," he said, snapping his fingers.

Arden hesitantly walked down into the shop and asked, "What was that about?"

Buffoh rolled his eyes. "Nothin', it was just one of my friend's sister's aunt's siblings... four times removed—not important. Now, let's get movin'. I wanna be well outta' town before any more customers show up."

Arden scanned the shop, almost forgetting how cluttered and dusty it was.

"Unlikely," he said under his breath.

The two of them wasted no more time talking. They gathered their belongings, readied themselves for the journey, and left The Gribic's Eye.

For nearly a day and a half, they trekked through harsh wind and rain. Though the weather was awful, it was nothing compared to Buffoh's constant complaining. With each hill they climbed, field they crossed, and forest they ventured through, Buffoh couldn't resist lamenting about Anura's festival and how he'd be missing his favorite dish, roasted omen flies glazed in snail slime.

On their second afternoon, they trudged through the Marsh of Lear. Buffoh had been recounting a particularly strange adventure about the time he'd gone to Jenoha Desert and encountered the Hobs of Wicknott: cruel beings known for feeding lost travelers to their bloodthirsty beasts.

Arden's interest in the story was minimal at best, but he pretended to listen anyway. While giving the occasional half-hearted response to Buffoh's outrageous account, the boy took in the sights of the swampy terrain before them.

The Marsh of Lear was a dreary place: a wide flatland with towering dead seagrass and shallow streams that slithered far off into the foggy woods.

It was so far from the comforts of Noakwood Hollow that it made Arden feel very out of his element. His mind began to wander, imagining if he'd ever be able to go back to his old acorn home in those tranquil woods.

An upward change in Buffoh's tone suddenly drew Arden's attention.

"Hey, kid! Did ya hear me?" the man asked.

"Sorry," Arden replied, realizing the Leptoid had finished his tale and was now addressing him directly. "What was your question?"

Buffoh grumbled. "I said, ya must do somethin' for a livin', right? I mean, judgin' by the amount of chip ya gave me to come out here and all."

Arden's hands tensed. How would Buffoh, a shopkeeper, take the news of him being a thief? This probably wasn't the best time to disclose *that* bit of information. And with rumors of his secret stone flying around Mogoroth, it's possible Buffoh might've heard something. Arden would be a fool to mention anything that hinted toward the matter but struggled to come up with a good answer.

"Oh," he said hesitantly. "I'm a borrower—a trader of sorts."

"Ah," Buffoh replied. "So, a thief."

The boy's jaw hung open, but no words came out.

Well, so much for keeping that under wraps, he thought.

Buffoh laughed. "Don't sweat it, kid. Ya secret's safe with me."

Relieved, Arden exhaled the air that had been trapped in his lungs.

Buffoh snickered some more, then said, "Trust me, I've known *quite* a few thieves in my lifetime—and pirates too. See, back when I lived in Mogoroth, half my pals were crooks and—"

"Oh, of course," Arden interjected, throwing a hand to his forehead. "You're from Mogoroth! I knew your accent sounded familiar."

Buffoh stopped in his tracks and spun around quickly.

"Whoa, hold on!" he exclaimed. "*You're* the one with the accent."

Arden shook his head.

"I'm not the... Never mind," he said. "How long ago did you live there?"

"Oh, way back, kid," Buffoh replied, resuming his walk. "My mother owned a little boot shop there, but after a while, the competition became too much for her. Besides, she was gettin' way too old to run the place by herself."

"Well, weren't you there to help her?"

"Yeah, I did. I sold the shop, took the money, and got into the guidin' business," Buffoh said as he hopped over a small stream. "Oh, and watch ya step there."

Then he unsheathed his giant scissor blade like a sword and began to cut a path through the overgrown grass.

"But what about you?" he asked. "Ya got anybody back home? Any family?"

Gord's image swept across Arden's mind. The boy hadn't thought of him in days.

"I have a father. Well... at least I did until I left him. But I kind of had no choice," he replied in a somber tone. "I'm just hoping after this journey, I'll be able to see him again."

"I take it ya's get along well?" Buffoh asked.

"Yes, actually. We do everything together: fish, forage, and even watch the sunset once in a while."

Buffoh paused, chuckling with a somewhat serious expression. "Yeah? I wish I could say the same thing 'bout my father. He was one of those no-good-muck-eaters, as my mother put it. He never cared for me or her very much. Then, one day outta the blue, he left us to fend for ourselves."

"That's horrible," Arden said. "I mean, I can't imagine *what* my life would be like without my father."

Buffoh shrugged. "Eh. In my case, it was for the best. That's what I always tell myself. Sometimes ya gotta cut out the people that are hurtin' ya, even if they *are* ya family."

Continuing onward, the boy and his guide reached the edge of the marsh and had now entered a dark wilderness.

Buffoh went on to say something, but Arden was far too absorbed with his own thoughts. Doubts of whether or not he should've left Gord and Mugz weighed on him. Thinking back now, it seemed more like a betrayal than a favor. He imagined that morning they'd woken up to find him gone. What fears ran through their minds? It was a pain that Arden didn't even have the heart to envision.

Buffoh's voice snaked its way back into the boy's ears mid-sentence, "...And then we heard that old fool was eaten by a yip. Serves him right for how he treated us."

Arden raised a brow. "I'm sorry—a yip? What's a yip?"

Buffoh scoffed. "Uh, they're only the most dangerous creatures in all of Cynorrum, kid. Picture this—a duck bill crammed with giant teeth, a neck longer than a tree, and its whole body covered in green vines. They're terrifyin'— known for devourin' everythin' in their path, especially Leptoids, like me." Buffoh shivered at the thought. "Ya better hope we don't come across one 'cause the swamp is crawlin' with 'em."

Arden put little trust in the Leptoid's description, given the man's previous ignorance about the proper usage of a cooking pot. But considering all of the other horrific legends about the swamp, he couldn't dismiss the possibility that yips might be dangerous.

"I take it you've encountered a lot of them before?" Arden asked.

Buffoh scratched the protruding pores on his forehead. "Well—actually. No."

"What? Then how do you know if they even exist—"

Buffoh froze in place.

"Wait a minute!" he shouted, pausing their conversation to point at various spots in the forest. "These trees, those rocks, that hill—I think I remember a shortcut up there: a travelers' tunnel that can take us to the Weepin' Meadow. It'd be the quickest route to Mukkis."

Arden peered up the tall, dark ridge. Though its crooked trees were dead and covered in webs, the area appeared much more overgrown than the rest of the woods.

"Are you sure?" he asked skeptically. "It seems a bit unsafe. Maybe we could go around it instead."

"Ay! We can't go around it," Buffoh grumbled. "Unless ya don't mind bein' flattened by boulders four times our size. Trust me, there's nothin' round this hill except mountains and rocky trails. We could get lost for days. I don't know about *you*, kid, but I ain't rock-climbin'. So, we better play it safe and go my way."

The Elf nodded in agreement, and they began to embark up the hill. However, within minutes, Buffoh stopped in his tracks again. He turned to Arden and quickly threw all of his belongings into the boy's arms.

"Hold my stuff, kid. I gotta take a leak," he said before running into the thick trees, leaving no room for protest.

Arden huffed. There he stood, on some creepy hill, by himself, holding all of Buffoh's possessions.

"What am I even doing?" he muttered to himself, gazing at the mountain of items in his arms.

A branch snapped behind him.

Arden jolted backward, then turned to look.

One of the bushes nearby rustled a bit like something was crawling around inside. Perhaps it was a small animal. Arden *was* rather hungry, and he hadn't had a proper meal in days.

Curious to investigate, the boy placed Buffoh's belongings to the ground as quietly as he could, then pulled his slingshot from his satchel. He slowly took a step back from the bush, placing a sharp rock into the weapon's band.

Another snap echoed.

Arden pulled the slingshot back and released his grip. The small stone flew straight into the gaps of the shrub's branches.

"Ow!" a voice cried.

The plant shuffled in pain.

Arden stepped back in shock. He'd assumed it was just an animal hiding there, not a person. For a moment, the boy felt guilty, but maybe it was just Buffoh playing a prank on him. Just then, a paranoid thought crossed his mind. Could this have been someone following him? Perhaps it was that hook-handed scavenger or, worse—the Or'Ackin sorceress.

Unwilling to take any chances, Arden drew another rock from the ground and readied his aim once more.

CHAPTER 11

A LOST TRAVELER

"Who's there? Show yourself," Arden said sternly.

No answer came from within the shrub.

"I won't ask again. Come out right now," the boy demanded, drawing the band of his weapon even tighter.

Arden was seconds from letting go, barely holding the string by his fingernails, when the voice suddenly shouted, "Don't!"

Arden halted but kept his aim steady.

The bush's leaves began to shuffle, and a girl emerged from its shroud with haste.

This was no hunter but a young Elf like him. A honey-tinted vest sat over the girl's tattered dress, and a long auburn braid cascaded down her left shoulder. She seemed frazzled but alert, swiftly grabbing a stone dagger from her belt.

"Who are you?" she asked from a distance, keeping her blade out in defense. "What do you want?"

"What do I want? Why are *you* following me?"

"I could ask you the same thing!" the girl said, her green eyes glaring. "You're the one who just launched a rock at my shoulder."

"Well, maybe I wouldn't have if you weren't being so suspicious and hiding in a bush."

The girl stepped back further. "I wasn't hiding. I—"

"Oh really, then you were just sitting in a shrub all day—is that it?"

"As a matter of fact, I was."

"Who rests in a bush?" Arden asked, still skeptical.

The girl scoffed, then continued, "Listen, I've been traveling for days. I was just taking a moment to rest which, no thanks to you, is over now."

The boy lowered his weapon, slightly embarrassed at the fact that he just pelted some innocent girl with a rock.

"Oh, well, I didn't know that... but what else was I supposed to think except that you were following me?"

"We've never met. Is there a reason I should?" the girl asked.

"No, but I..." Arden hesitated. "Perhaps this is all a misunderstanding," he admitted. "I didn't mean to hurt you. It's just hard to know who you can trust."

The girl's uneasy breaths subsided, and her posture loosened.

"Agreed," she replied, slowly bringing the stone knife down to her side and placing a hand on her hip.

There was an awkward moment of silence between them as they stared at one another.

"Um... so what are you doing out here anyway? If you don't mind me asking," Arden inquired.

The girl sighed.

"I've been trying to get to this city, Haroon—to meet my sister—but she didn't give the best directions on how to get there. Honestly, I think I've been going in circles," she admitted. "You wouldn't happen to know how to get there, would you?"

Arden scratched his chin.

"I'm sorry," he said. "To be honest, I've never even heard of Haroon before, but—"

He quickly paused as a heavy shadow hobbled out of the woods beside the girl, followed by the sound of a dozen tumbling rocks. It was Buffoh making his elegant return. The Leptoid's gaze was fixed on the lumpy ground beneath his feet.

"*But...* maybe my guide could tell you," Arden continued, pointing to the man approaching her left. "That's him coming over now."

Buffoh grunted his way down to Arden, completely unaware of the Elven girl standing beside him.

"Kid, I gotta tell ya," he said. "That was the longest leak I ever—"

The Leptoid came to a sudden halt, finally noticing the lost stranger. "Ay! Who are *you*?"

"Buffoh, this is..." the boy started, but his words trailed off. He realized he hadn't gotten the girl's name. "I'm sorry. I don't think we've introduced ourselves."

"Oh, right," the girl said. "I'm Vee."

"Vee!" Arden repeated with a nod. "Well, I'm Arden, and this *charming* Leptoid here is Buffoh."

"Vee?" Buffoh asked with a chuckle. "Vee's a letter, lady, not a name."

The girl rolled her eyes.

"Anyway," Arden continued, glaring at the Leptoid. "As I was trying to say before, Buffoh practically knows everything about these woods. Surely, *he* can tell you where Haroon is."

"Haroon?" Buffoh asked, his brow furrowing. "Pfft! I haven't heard of that place in ages. Why would ya wanna go there?"

"I'm meeting someone," Vee said, fiddling with a stone piercing at the bottom of her pointed ear. "A family member, actually. As I told Arden here earlier, my sister gave me terrible directions and I got lost. I've never been through this part of the forest before, but Arden mentioned you might know how to get there."

Buffoh crossed his arms and grumbled, "Fine. I'll give ya directions, but they ain't gonna matter. Haroon is past the borders of Mukkis, which means ya'd have to trek through the swamp to get there."

"Alright... So, I'll just go through the swamp then," Vee said with passive aggression.

Arden could tell this girl didn't have a clue what she was up against: the dangers of the swamp. And he would've bet all of his remaining possessions that Buffoh was gearing up to rant about how horrible the place was.

Sure enough, the Leptoid turned to him slowly, appalled at the girl's lack of knowledge. Buffoh's pupils grew wide, and a little hiccup left his excited throat.

"Here we go," Arden moaned, placing a palm to his face.

"It ain't just some swamp," Buffoh declared dramatically, his arms flailing. "It's *Blackwater* Swamp! I mean—not to scare ya—but it's the most treacherous place in Cynorrum. It's like a living being, capable of sensing ya fears and making them real. Nobody gets through that place, not without a guide anyway." Buffoh gestured a hand toward Arden, then continued, "Just like the kid here. He'd never survive alone out there without me. And luckily for *you*, lady, we're headin' to the swamp ourselves."

"No, thanks. I'll just go around the swamp instead," Vee replied.

"Oh, there's no goin' around it. Blackwater stretches from the Terric Ocean to the Sleepin' Sea—coast to coast of Mukkis."

"So what are you saying, toad?" the girl asked dryly.

Buffoh pompously inspected his mud-caked fingernails, picking at the dirt.

"Well, I'm sayin' if ya wanna get to Haroon, ya gonna need me," he replied, exposing his big yellow teeth with a cheesy grin.

Vee passed a phony smile back. "I think I'll be just *fine* without you."

"Are you sure?" Arden asked. "I mean, I know what Buffoh's saying sounds insane—and I thought the same thing at first—but he *seems* to know what he's talking about, so far. I've also heard from others that the swamp can be a deadly place. You might want to consider going there with a guide."

Vee shook her head with a thin veil of irritation, but took a moment to ponder the suggestion. Scanning over the two travelers once more, she bit her cheek.

"Well, Buffoh, if everything you said is true... then maybe you're right," she replied, gazing at the man with reluctance.

He smirked at her obvious discontent.

"So? Will you guide me to Haroon?" Vee muttered through her clenched teeth.

"Sure! Of course! Yeah," Buffoh said. "But it's gonna cost ya."

Vee's eyes widened. "Uh... I don't have any money."

"Well, then... ya on your own," the Leptoid replied calmly.

"But I—"

"If ya gonna follow us, then I'm gonna need some chip or somethin' to trade, at least. And if ya can't provide either of those, then I can't help ya."

The girl looked over her person in search of something to barter with.

"Wait, I could give you one of my daggers," she said, presenting the stone knife in her palm.

Buffoh squinted. "Hmm. Nah! Worthless."

Vee placed her dagger back into its holster.

"Well, how about my earrings?" she asked, showing off their rare, marble-like exterior.

Buffoh expressed little interest in the girl's second offering.

"What about that thing around ya neck?" he asked, his attention drawn to the amber gem glistening beneath her collar.

"You mean my pendant?" she asked, clutching the necklace.

Buffoh nodded.

"Yep," he said, waving a finger. "I want that. Gimme that, and ya got yaself a guide."

Vee held the necklace close to her chest. "No... you can't have this. I'm sorry."

Buffoh scoffed.

"Then the deal's off, lady," he said, picking up his bags from the grass and turning to Arden. "Let's go, kid. We're wastin' our time here."

The Leptoid started up the hill.

Arden looked back and forth between Buffoh and Vee. Grumbling, he jogged up toward the old toad and matched his pace.

"Should we really just leave her like this?" he asked.

"Not ya concern, kid," Buffoh replied, continuing to march. "This Elf girl ain't got anything to offer—and that's *her* problem."

"Well, that's a little cold," Arden said.

Buffoh laughed. "I'm a Leptoid, pal. It's in my blood. And let's not forget, ya ain't payin' me to be nice here."

Arden glanced back at the girl down the hill.

Vee stood there, still holding onto the pendant close to her chest. She turned back toward the road behind her, seemingly in deep thought.

She must've been preparing to go back the way she came, Arden surmised as he continued to follow his guide. He knew what it was like to be lost and out of options. And if not for the money he had on hand, Buffoh would've surely left him in the dust, just like this girl.

He brought his gaze forward, trying to bury the guilt that began to rise, but a voice cut through it, "Hold up!"

Arden and Buffoh came to a labored halt, watching Vee approach them.

"Fine," she said. "I'll give you my pendant."

"Now, that's more like it," Buffoh replied, merrily placing his hand straight out toward the girl. "Hand it over."

Vee quickly untied her necklace and dropped the pendant into the man's hand, her stare fixed on him.

"Are we good now?" she asked, crossing her arms.

"Yep," Buffoh said, pocketing the item in his leather vest. "See? That wasn't so hard, was it?"

Arden couldn't help but notice the heartbreak in Vee's eyes as she reluctantly parted with the necklace. It was clear that it held sentimental value. Perhaps it was a gift from someone dear to her. He felt a pang of sympathy, but as he watched Buffoh tuck it away, Arden's own conflicted thoughts surfaced.

Was it really any different from what he did—stealing for profit? In the past, Arden had been able to distance himself from the consequences of his actions. He had never been present to witness the moment when his victims realized their belongings were gone. It was easy to justify his actions as survival, a means to support himself and his father in their secluded home.

But now, standing there and seeing the impact on Vee, it all felt more immediate—more real. He couldn't ignore the guilt creeping in, knowing that his thievery had caused distress and loss to others. It was a stark reminder that behind every stolen item was a memory, a history, and a person who cherished it.

Breaking Arden from his thoughts, Buffoh pressed on with a triumphant shout.

"To Blackwater Swamp it is! Oh, and by the way, lady," he said, "ya may wanna watch out for yips."

Vee raised an eyebrow, casting a puzzled glance at Arden for an explanation.

The boy groaned, feeling a mix of irritation and resignation.

"Don't even ask," he said.

CHAPTER 12

THE SHORTCUT

Buffoh led the way with confidence as they reached the top of the hill. Before them sat a cave surrounded by gnarled trees and dead vines. Massive cobwebs dangled from its circular entrance. It appeared this passage had been abandoned since Buffoh's last visit.

"A tunnel?" Vee asked, looking ahead at the ominous route. "This seems risky."

Arden glanced over, discreetly gesturing for the girl to stop voicing her concerns. He could already feel Buffoh's rage beginning to build.

"Oh, great!" the Leptoid exclaimed, slapping his thigh. "Another one who thinks they know everything. I'll say this one more time, then. The paths around this hill have hazardous landslides, so goin' through this tunnel is our safest option."

Vee huffed.

"It's not just the safety that concerns me—it's that smell," she replied in a nasal voice, pinching her nose shut. "Has the tunnel always smelt this bad?"

Buffoh turned to the cave in a swift motion, scratching his head.

"Uh, I think so," he said. "It's probably somethin' to do with not gettin' any sunlight. Makes it a little musty in there. Nothin' to worry about, though. Quit the paranoia."

The old Leptoid dropped his overstuffed bags onto the nearest boulder and began rummaging through them.

"Now, before we head in, we gotta make a torch," Buffoh continued, pulling out a ragged piece of fabric stained with gray oil. "Make yaself useful, kid. Hand me that stick by ya leg there."

Arden picked up a very straight and stubby branch resting beside him, then handed it to the man.

"Alright. There we go!" Buffoh said, tying the cloth securely to the stick. He reached into the bag again and retrieved the spark bark the boy had traded with him earlier. "And for the finishin' touch, a lil' bit of this should do the trick."

He chipped off a small chunk of the bark, and within seconds, orange sparks flew out, engulfing the fabric in a brilliant flame.

"What is that stuff?" Vee asked.

"It's called spark bark," Arden explained, gazing at the fiery embers of the torch. "Buffoh says it's super rare to come by."

The Leptoid fanned the remaining spark bark out like a match, raised the torch high, and faced the two weary Elves.

"Ya ready?" he asked.

Arden and Vee peered into the gloomy tunnel ahead with uncertainty. Neither responded.

"Good," Buffoh replied, marching into the tunnel. "We're goin' in!"

The two teenagers watched as the Leptoid bravely walked into the darkness and disappeared. Arden looked at Vee, sensing she was just as nervous as he was.

Approaching the cave carefully, Arden could feel a cold air flow out from within it. A chill ran down his spine, but whether it was from the gust or the fear of entering, it didn't seem to make a difference. He had no choice but to continue onward.

Inside the tunnel, there was no light to signify its end. Buffoh's torch was the only source of illumination, surrounding them in a bubble that revealed the cave's bumpy walls.

For a while, they strolled through in silence. Arden sensed an unease in Vee, still lingering from earlier.

"So, where are you from? Aramore?" he asked her.

"Aramore? No, I'm not from there. I'm from Rook, a trading town west of here."

"A trading town?" the boy asked. "You mean like Mogoroth?"

"Not exactly," Vee replied, keeping her gaze fixed on Buffoh's torch ahead. "It's smaller than that. Much smaller. Rook is a diverse place, though. We have a few Noamins, Haggarts, Elves—sometimes the occasional Leptoid."

"Huh, I didn't know there were other markets around," Arden mused.

Vee continued, "Well, I wouldn't really call it a market. Rook is more like... if you took twenty stores and dropped them along a road."

"Less chaotic than Mogoroth, I'm sure. Must be nice," Arden said.

Vee shrugged. "Sort of, but Rook isn't anything to brag about. It's a shabby town with some... *unkind* people, if I may say. To be honest, that's why I don't mind leaving to meet my sister at Haroon. At least I'd be able to get away from there for a little while. But what about you? Where are you and the toad from?"

Buffoh continued ahead, seemingly unfazed by the two Elves' conversation.

"Well, Buffoh is from Anura village, and I'm from Noak—"Arden started but cut himself short, "Aramore, actually!"

"Oh. So, why are you going to the swamp, then?" Vee asked. "Based on how treacherous you made it sound earlier, it seems like the last place anybody would want to be—unless they *had* to go through it, of course, like I do."

The nerves in Arden's back tightened. He knew he shouldn't mention his quest to find a legendary witch but couldn't think of a good excuse on the spot.

"I... have to meet someone there," he said meekly, "and Buffoh agreed to guide me."

"I see. And who is it you know in a swamp?" Vee asked.

Arden chuckled nervously, taking a step away from her. "Uh... just an old friend of sorts."

Before the girl could delve further into the conversation, Buffoh spun around and said, "Ay! I hate to cut ya's short, but we should stop here for the night."

Arden let out a sigh of relief. For once, he was rather grateful Buffoh had intervened. Any more questions about his personal life and he might've said something too revealing.

Vee, however, wasn't so thrilled with the idea.

"Stop here?" she questioned. "I didn't expect us to spend the night. I thought we'd be walking straight through this place in one go."

"Listen, lady," Buffoh snapped, waving the torch with every word. "I've been travelin' all day, my feet are hurtin', and I gotta get some rest."

Arden agreed, suddenly aware of his own fatigue. "Maybe Buffoh's right. We *could* stop and rest for a bit. We don't know how much further this tunnel goes. And besides, my feet are killing me, too."

Vee sighed, shaking her head.

"Some travelers *you* are," she muttered.

As they settled in for the night, Buffoh planted the torch securely in the center of the cave to provide equal lighting. Then he walked ahead and declared his resting spot with enthusiasm.

"Yup, this side's good for me!" he said, dropping his bags to the ground.

The Leptoid drew a pillow from his belongings. Though filthy and misshapen, Buffoh made use of it anyway. With a smile, he propped it up against the cave wall and took a rest.

Arden shook his head and leaned against a slanted side of the tunnel, tucking one knee up toward his chest and using his satchel as a cushion. No matter how he shifted, he couldn't find comfort. The cave floor was damp and lumpy.

Curious to see how Vee was faring, he glanced in her direction. The girl was tossing and turning, cursing to herself in shrill whispers.

Arden couldn't help but chuckle at her almost comical display.

"It might be more comfortable to just sleep standing up," he said.

"I guess so," Vee replied, continuing to fidget.

Arden smirked, glancing at the girl one last time—until something unusual grabbed his attention: a streak of red pooling atop her thigh.

"Your leg!" he whispered. "It's bleeding."

Vee sat straight and noticed the crimson stain saturating the wraps above her knee. "Oh... don't worry. It's fine."

Arden approached her and knelt to inspect the wound. It appeared she had used one of the cloth wraps from her pants to make a bandage, but it wasn't properly tied—the bleeding hadn't stopped.

"That looks pretty bad," he remarked.

Vee examined herself in the torchlight, a hint of nervousness in her voice. "Does it?"

Arden nodded. "I can help."

"Don't. I'm fine."

"Are you sure?" the boy asked. "Because I think—"

"No! No. It's alright," Vee replied sharply.

Arden studied the girl, unconvinced by her assurances. "But it must be causing you pain. And I know enough about wounds to tell you that if this doesn't get treated, it'll get infected."

Vee remained silent. Hesitating, she began to untie the wrap, rolling up her pant leg with visible discomfort. She paused, unable to continue.

"I don't remember you getting injured," Arden said. "How did this happen?"

"Yesterday, while I was traveling," Vee replied, "I fell into a thorn bush. It cut me up worse than I thought. I figured covering it would stop the bleeding, but clearly it hasn't."

The girl winced for a moment.

Arden walked back over to his satchel and grabbed something from inside.

"Here," he said, carrying over a clump of pink and green

leaves shaped like tongues. "I think I've got just the thing."

"How's that pile of leaves going to help me exactly?" Vee asked.

"They're not just any leaves. This is ferry tongue."

"Fairy what?"

"Not 'fairy'—ferry," he said, holding the herbs up for her to see. "I've applied this on many cuts before. Not mine, really. I've always been a fast healer. But I've used it for my family lots of times. Trust me, it works."

Vee inspected the leaves, then peeked up at him with uncertainty.

The boy nodded toward her wound, signaling for her to fully reveal it.

Taking a few deep breaths, she lifted the rest of her bandages away from the gash.

Arden cringed at the sight.

Dried blood had collected in the wound, yet it still seemed fresh. The skin around it was red and swollen.

Arden was amazed she had endured such pain without a word. He gulped, clearing his throat.

"Wow. A *shrub* did this to you?"

Vee fell silent, then jokingly replied, "It was a really sharp shrub."

Arden chuckled, and the girl smiled back.

"Listen," he continued, "chew this ferry tongue into a paste and apply it directly to the cut. Now, I won't lie, it's going to sting at first—maybe a lot—but that only means it's working."

Vee nodded.

Arden handed her the leaves before heading back to his resting spot. As he settled, she called his name in a whisper.

Turning back to her, he asked, "What is it?"

"Thank you," Vee said sincerely.

Arden smiled at her gratitude, then curled up, attempting to get comfy.

As the travelers slept in the secluded cave, a much livelier event took place at Anura village: The Festival of the Flies. Leptoids from far and wide had gathered to bask in the splendor of this wonderful evening. Musicians played fiddles and drums, children frolicked about, and everyone engaged in traditional challenges and games.

The villagers' delight filled the air until a ghostly wind rushed through the town, forcing everyone to a rapid halt. Lanterns blew out, buffet tables toppled over, and jars filled with brown omen flies crashed down into the dirt. People ceased their conversations as the wind came to an eerie standstill.

Frozen in the ominous gloom, the Leptoids' gazes instinctively aimed at the village's main entrance in unison. They watched as a blue cloud crept in from the forest road, twisting and swirling as it approached the archway. With a

114

deep hum, it climbed high into the air, forming a thick wall just beyond the gates as if forbidden to enter.

The Leptoids murmured and whispered, questioning if what they were seeing was real.

The sound of monstrous footsteps broke the silence, resonating from within the mist. A low growl trembled, gnawing in the Leptoids' ears.

Finally, the source of the haunting sounds came into view: a massive, hunched gringore mounted by a shadowy woman.

The villagers gasped.

An Or'Ackin sorceress was in their midst—her glowing white eyes leering at them as her wild curls and cape were stirred by an unseen wind.

Her vicious and raspy voice suddenly rumbled through the village, "WHERE IS HE?"

Terror-stricken, the villagers remained silent, unsure of whom the cruel sorceress was referring to.

"W-who is it you seek?" stuttered an old Leptoid.

"THE BOY! THE ELF!"

The Or'Ackin's angry voice grew louder, rattling Anura's main gate.

"This is but a simple Leptoid village," the old man replied timidly. "There are no Elves here—"

A long gray whip lashed out from the fog with a horrible snap. The townsfolk jumped back in fear.

"LIES," the sorceress yelled, bringing the whip back to her side. "BRING HIM TO ME NOW."

Paralyzed by terror, the Leptoids stayed quiet.

"Very well," the Or'Ackin said in a chillingly calm voice. She unhooked the boomerang from her belt and held it out wide. "If you will not speak—THEN YOU SHALL BURN!"

Her weapon began to glow red. The Leptoids could feel its intense heat as it smoked in her hands. The Or'Ackin prepared to strike, rapidly raising the boomerang high above her head.

"Wait!" a villager shouted.

The sorceress froze in her stance as a middle-aged Leptoid stepped out from the crowd. It was Lonny, Buffoh's neighbor.

"North," Lonny said firmly. "He's traveling north."

The villagers stood, perplexed, wondering how Lonny had gained such knowledge.

"WHERE?" the sorceress demanded.

Lonny sighed. "Blackwater Swamp. He left over two days ago."

In an instant, the glow of the sorceress's boomerang dimmed, and she placed the weapon back into the holster.

The townsfolk exhaled a collective sigh of relief. But then, the mist around the woman began to twist and coil.

Another powerful gust swept across the village, parting the crowd in half.

When the wind subsided, the villagers arose from the ground, scanning the area for the Or'Ackin sorceress. To their astonishment, she and the gringore had disappeared. The only evidence left of their presence was a fallen sign at the end of the road—a sign that read "The Gribic's Eye."

CHAPTER 13

AT THE END OF THE TUNNEL

A beam of light shined onto Arden's face as he slept in the cold tunnel. It was barely the size of his fist but large enough to warm his cheek. He flung an eye open and slowly sat up from the rough ground, his back aching. The torch from last night had long since burned out, leaving the travelers in almost complete darkness. But to the boy's surprise, a distant speck of sunlight hovered just beyond the void of the cave. The exit! It couldn't have been more than a couple of hours away.

"Hey, wake up!" Arden exclaimed, jumping to his feet.

Buffoh plugged his ear holes to drown out the disturbance. "Grr! What is it with you and wakin' me up so damn early?"

"Come on, get up," Arden replied. "See? Daylight. We're almost out of this tunnel."

Vee awoke and sprung to her knees.

"Really?" she asked groggily, rubbing her eyes.

Buffoh hobbled up and squinted at the small point of light.

"Huh, would ya look at that?" he asked.

Arden felt around the cave for his satchel. Once found, he threw it over his shoulder and headed for the welcoming sun.

"Let's go, you old toad. Grab your things," he urged.

Buffoh grunted. "Hold ya crogs, kid."

As the Leptoid leaned over to gather his belongings, his hand brushed against something unfamiliar.

"Wait, what is this?" he asked, feeling its soft exterior.

"That's my leg," Vee answered dryly.

"Oh," Buffoh replied. "It's kinda dark in here."

Eager to get moving, Arden assisted the man in retrieving his items, carelessly grabbing whatever he could find and tossing it into Buffoh's heavy bags.

"Hold on a second, kid! There's an order to how I pack this stuff," Buffoh exclaimed, but Arden was already marching for the exit.

"Shouldn't we light another torch?" Vee asked from behind the group.

"Nah, we don't need one," Buffoh declared. "We'll use that lil' bit of sunlight to guide us."

"But I don't think that's enough—"

"It's fine! Sheesh," the tired Leptoid snapped. "We can't possibly get lost in here. It's a straight path all the way through. Now, let's get movin'. The Weepin' Meadow is just on the other side of this thing."

As the trio pressed onward, the light at the end of the tunnel grew larger and brighter. But with every step, the vulgar aroma of rot intensified, and the uneven floor they walked upon became stickier.

"Is it just me, or is the smell of this place getting worse?" Vee asked, pinching her nose shut.

"I think it's just *you*," Buffoh replied, marching ahead with confidence.

Arden shivered, just as nauseated by the odor.

An unsettling crunch began to accompany their every footstep.

"No, I think she's right," he said, continuing forward. "And what's this cracking sound?"

Buffoh groaned. "It's just some sticks, kid. We're fine. Keep it movin'."

Arden tried to ignore the noise but couldn't shake that something was amiss.

"I know the sound of sticks breaking," he said, stopping abruptly, "and these definitely aren't sticks."

Reaching out his hand, the boy continued, "Buffoh! Throw me the spark bark I gave you."

"My spark bark?" the Leptoid questioned. "No way, pal."

"Just give it to me," Arden demanded.

"Fine! Here," Buffoh grumbled, angrily fishing the spark bark from his vest and tossing it over.

Arden crouched down, hovering his knees just above the cave floor. Holding the bark low and steady, he snapped off a small chunk, and bright embers burst forth, illuminating the scene.

The boy's eyes widened.

Vee gasped.

Buffoh croaked.

Dozens of carcasses lined the ground beneath the travelers' feet. Covered in a shiny, black slime, the bones of previous beings and animals were adhered to every surface. Suddenly, the reason for the stench was apparent. These creatures were being dissolved.

Arden and the others screamed in terror.

The slime began to engulf their shoes, too thick to move through and too solid to shake off.

Vee grabbed her daggers, attempting to scrape off the acidic gunk, but it clung to her with an unyielding grip. The more she clawed at it, the tighter it squeezed.

Arden followed suit, trying to pry the muck away with his bare hands, but it stung to the touch, like boiling water.

"Ouch! It burns," he shouted. "Buffoh! What is this stuff?"

The Leptoid held his bags high, protecting them from the flesh-eating slime.

"I don't know!" he cried out. "But the tunnel must've gotten infected or somethin'."

"Well, that's just great," Vee snapped, still unable to free her feet from the gunk. "How are we supposed to get out of this, then?"

"Oh, I'll tell ya how," Buffoh yelled, gazing toward the tunnel's exit. "Help! Help! Somebody help!"

Arden and Vee joined the man's desperate wails as the slime continued to crawl up their socks. The boy could feel an intense heat building as it began to dissolve his shoes and blister his shins. He scouted around for something to aid in their struggle, but it was no use.

Just then, an enormous shadow eclipsed the sunlight at the cave's end.

"What's that now?" Vee asked, noticing the figure.

Buffoh turned to look, squinting at the tunnel's exit. His pupils dilated as a terrible realization struck.

"It's—it's a yip!" he screamed. "We're doomed!"

The travelers shrieked in fear as the beast charged straight into the tunnel for them.

Arden tried his best to escape, continuing to tear as much slime from his feet as he could. If not for the pure adrenaline, the burning sensation on his hands might've been too much to bear. Clenching his teeth and giving a yell in desperation, he was finally able to rip some of the acidic gunk from his shoes, but it was too late.

The beast had reached them.

Arden felt a meaty hand grab the back of his shirt and lift him straight out of the slime with ease. The vile substance writhed from the forceful pull, jumping clean off his body and back to the cave floor.

Before he could react, Arden was tossed over the shoulder of the shadowy behemoth, along with Vee and Buffoh. Wind rushed past the boy's face as the monster started barreling back out of the tunnel.

Blinded by the darkness, and still in shock, Arden pictured Gord's face in the void, probably still out there somewhere, struggling to find him. It was a face he'd probably never see again, but as the daylight grew nearer, he realized his vision of Gord was no daydream at all. Gaining his senses back, he could see the Ogre clear as day now, panting for breath. This was no monster hauling them toward the exit—it was Gord!

A wave of relief washed over the boy, but Vee and Buffoh were still busy screaming for their lives. Arden tried to tell them they'd just been saved but couldn't find the strength to speak.

With a mighty leap, Gord burst out of the tunnel, landing heavily on his feet just beyond the exit of the cave.

They were free.

The Ogre placed the three travelers down at the foot of some towering boulders. Overwhelmed by the sight of his lost son, Gord wrapped the boy in a warm embrace.

Arden had never been more relieved to see his father. Ignoring the pain of his blistered shins, he hugged back as tightly as he could.

"I'm sorry I left," he choked. "I missed you so much."

"Oh, kid!" Buffoh screamed, clenching his eyes shut as he latched onto Vee's waist for comfort. "That thing's crushin' him!"

"No, Buffoh. It's alright," Arden said as Gord released him and smiled.

Vee sighed in relief, seeing that the Ogre wasn't a threat. She panned down at the Leptoid clinging to her side with disgust.

"Get off me," the girl said, shoving Buffoh away. "Arden's fine. Stop your screaming."

Buffoh peeked an eye open to see for himself, slowly realizing there was nothing to be afraid of.

"Oh," he replied, dusting himself off to appear composed.

Gord turned his head back, put two fingers to his lips, and gave a good whistle.

From the top of the cave behind him, a small furry head with two black horns popped up.

"Mugz!" Arden exclaimed.

The mugget jumped down from the hill and scurried onto the boy's shoulder, nuzzling into his neck with joy.

"I missed you too," Arden said, petting the creature's pink ears. "Vee, Buffoh, I want you to meet my family. This is my father, Gord, and this little rascal here is Mugz."

The two travelers stared at the peculiar group with welcoming but confused eyes. Gord and Mugz returned a similar gaze.

"Whoa, hold on a second, kid," Buffoh remarked. "I don't remember ya sayin' ya father was an Ogre."

Arden's smile fell flat as he moved in front of Gord like a protective barrier. "Uh... is there something wrong with that?"

"No, no!" Buffoh said, taking note of the two massive teeth protruding from the Ogre's lower jaw. "It's just when ya described him yesterday—I was thinkin' of someone a little less... tall."

"I don't understand. I thought you lived in Aramore with the Elves," Vee remarked.

"Oh! I-I do," Arden said. "And so do Gord and Mugz. We all live there together."

Gord looked at his son, his brow furrowed.

Arden could almost feel his father's stare, so he discreetly put his hands behind his back and signed, *I'll explain later.*

Buffoh, still curious about the whole thing, rubbed his chin and asked Gord, "How did ya find us all the way out here, anyway? Aramore is pretty far. Ya must've been travelin' for days."

Arden turned to his father, eager to know the answer as

well. As per the request in his letter, Gord should've remained at his old village.

"Buffoh's got a point. How *did* you find us?"

Gord began to sign to the boy, *After you left, I couldn't help but feel guilty for letting you go off alone, so I—*

Buffoh quickly interjected, "Uhm, what's he doin'?"

Arden remembered that signing was something only he and Gord understood. Most others in Cynorrum were unaware of the language the Ogres created during their imprisonment in Havarria.

"Oh, Gord can't speak. We use hand gestures to communicate," Arden replied.

"Huh. WELL, WHAT'S HE SAYIN'!" Buffoh shouted.

Arden and Gord covered their ears.

"He can hear you, Buffoh," the boy snapped.

"Oh," the Leptoid muttered. "Sorry."

Arden turned back to his father, motioning for him to continue.

As Gord told the boy how he'd found them, Arden relayed the story to the group.

"Gord had Mugz follow my scent for days until they eventually ended up at the tunnel," he explained. "They were about to go through it, but Mugz smelled something foul coming from inside."

"Yep," Vee whispered under her breath, giving Buffoh a cold glare.

The Leptoid rolled his eyes. "Yeah, yeah. Keep goin', kid."

Arden proceeded, "So, they traveled around the hillside instead of venturing into the cave. They nearly got crushed by boulders as they went along the path, but luckily, Gord was able to avoid them."

"Ha! See that? I was right about the boulders," Buffoh gloated, nudging Vee's shoulder with a confident smirk.

The girl crossed her arms and looked away.

Arden continued, "It wasn't until morning that Gord reached the other end of the hill. He heard our screams echoing from the tunnel and... well, we know the rest."

Buffoh hesitated, then said, "Does that mean these two are comin' with us?"

Arden turned to Gord with hopeful eyes.

"Are you?" he asked, nervous that his father might still reject this whole quest to find a witch.

Gord scanned Buffoh and Vee, then turned back to his anxious son.

A deep sigh escaped the Ogre's lips, and he signed, *Well, not that I like the idea of you going to the swamp, but if it means having your questions answered, then I suppose...*

Gord paused before nodding in approval.

Arden's face lit up.

"They're coming with us," he announced to his new acquaintances.

"Well, if that's the case," Buffoh said as he slyly approached the boy and rubbed his fingertips together, "then ya gonna need to sweeten the deal, if ya know what I'm talkin' about."

Arden growled, shoving a hand into his satchel to retrieve his last bag of chip.

"How much?" he asked with contempt.

"Three hundred," Buffoh replied.

"Three hun—Fine. Whatever," Arden grumbled.

"Each," the Leptoid continued.

"Seriously? Give me a break already."

"Hey! I charge per head, and I'm countin' two more here," Buffoh said sternly, slapping his hand on every syllable.

The boy checked his remaining chip, but to his misfortune, he didn't have enough to cover Buffoh's fee.

"I only have three hundred *left*," Arden said regretfully.

Buffoh raised a judgmental brow but held a hand out in acceptance.

"Alright, fine," he said. "But ya gonna owe me the rest later."

"Deal," the boy said. He dropped the bag of chip into Buffoh's hand and watched it quickly disappear into the Leptoid's vest.

"Now, follow me," Buffoh said in a smug tone. He grabbed his bags and marched between the boulders that led to the northern path.

Vee trailed behind him, turning back to Arden as she walked.

"Here we go again," she said to the boy sarcastically.

Arden chuckled as he began to follow, but Gord grabbed his shoulder and motioned for him to stay back while the others went ahead.

Are you sure about this? he signed to the boy. I know Finn said Buffoh was trustworthy, but something seems off. And who's this Elf girl? Did Finn mention her too?

"Don't worry," Arden whispered. "Buffoh's strange, but I don't think he's dangerous. And Vee got lost trying to get to Haroon to meet her sister. Buffoh said he would take her there because it's just past the swamp. Once I find the witch, we'll probably just part ways. Trust me, I wouldn't have stayed with them if I thought they were a threat."

Gord still didn't seem convinced. *And if they discover you have a price on your head, or worse, they learn of your stone, what then? I can't risk losing you a second time.*

"You won't," Arden reassured him. "I haven't told them anything about our real identities. I only mentioned that you and I live in Aramore with the Elves and that I'm looking to meet an old friend at the swamp. To be honest, Buffoh barely paid attention when I said it, and Vee probably forgot by now."

Gord shook his head unsurely but gave in. *Alright, but I'll be keeping a very close eye on them, for both of our sakes.*

Arden nodded, slightly irritated that Gord was questioning his judgment, but he understood why. After all, the giant *did* just save them from flesh-eating slime.

"Great," the boy said. "Let's hurry. I don't want to fall too far behind."

Gord agreed.

They walked along the rocky path between the boulders until they reached Buffoh and Vee, who were waiting for them by a shallow cliffside.

"It's about time ya's showed up," the Leptoid said. He held out a hand toward the vast expanse of rolling hills and mountains behind him.

"Welcome to the Weepin' Meadow."

Chapter 14

THE WEEPING MEADOW

The sun shined brightly above the long mountain ranges that lined the east and the west. It was a serene and peaceful sight, a rare experience for Arden after what seemed like days of endless rain and clouds. His memory of the sun had nearly faded since he'd left home, but today, the sky was as blue as the sea.

Lush grass carpeted the rolling hills, sparkling streams scattered the ground, and clusters of trees gathered in small groves to mingle. Everything down to the dirt appeared harmonious and undisturbed. It was as if the mountains had kept this meadow shielded from all the perils of the world.

By dusk, Arden and his companions had crossed most of the meadow. Though the day had been cheerful, a weariness still clung to the travelers from the morning's tunnel incident. Despite their fatigue, Buffoh insisted on pressing forward without pause. So onward they went, their thoughts wandering and feet aching.

Upon walking up a shallow hill, their pace was abruptly interrupted by Mugz's loud barking. The little creature cowered closer to Arden's neck, whimpering at something behind them.

"What's the matter, girl?" Arden asked.

The mugget continued to stare south, barking and squeaking.

Arden turned around to see what had captured his pet's attention. He glanced at Vee and Gord, who'd been trailing behind him, but nothing seemed amiss. Then, just past his father's figure, Arden spotted something.

His eyes began to widen.

Billowing up from behind a mountain range was a jagged tower of smoke, slicing through the golden sunset.

"I wonder who made that," the boy mused.

Vee and Gord halted, drawing their attention to the peculiar sight behind their trail.

"Ay, what's the holdup?" Buffoh asked, realizing the sound of his travelers' footsteps had quickly stopped. He turned to them, ready to snap, but fell silent upon spotting the billowing cloud.

"Hey... I think we should keep moving," Vee said.

Buffoh scoffed.

"Ya mean 'cause of that?" he replied, pointing at the smoldering trail. "It's probably just some traveler makin' a campfire or somethin'."

That much was obvious, Arden thought.

Yet still, he questioned whose campsite it could've been. Just a day earlier, he and Buffoh had roamed those very woods and hadn't come across a single soul except for Vee. Suddenly, the Or'Ackin sorceress and the hook-handed scavenger flashed in Arden's mind. It could've been either of them who kindled that campfire, but standing around to find out which one wasn't an idea he was willing to entertain.

As the smoke loomed high above the open meadow, Arden turned away from the sunset as if the beauty of the sight had been tainted. Although this place seemed serene, it certainly didn't mean that danger couldn't find its way there. Not even its broad shield of mountains could keep these relentless hunters away.

Arden looked to Gord, trying to gauge his thoughts on the matter, but the boy's attention was drawn to Vee instead.

She stood there, staring at the ground, her left hand trembling.

Arden realized he wasn't the only one disturbed by the sight of the smoke.

"I agree with Vee. Let's keep going," he said. "Buffoh, how much further do we have anyway?"

The grumpy Leptoid turned to face their destination, squinting to discern the landscape beyond the hills.

A bleak forest lay hunched in the distance.

"Eh... not too much," Buffoh replied. "Once we get to those trees over there, we'll be enterin' Feverwood Forest— the border of Mukkis. It'd be a good place for us to camp for the night."

"Good," Arden said, glancing at his friends. "I think we all need that."

As they reached the outskirts of Feverwood Forest, Arden's fears were overshadowed by his curiosity about the grotesque woodlands.

A furry sleeve of moss encased every tree in sight, and although the ground had become muddier, there were no rain puddles to explain its sloshing. In the increasingly humid air, dozens of white and red garter beetles flew, buzzing with a high-pitched drone.

Buffoh had warned Arden that the further they ventured, the more marsh-like their surroundings would become. Now, walking through this terrain, Arden had no doubt that Blackwater Swamp was near.

By nightfall, the group had set up a campsite beneath the sickly green trees.

Arden watched as his father fell asleep against a wide log. Mugz had sprawled herself out over Gord's stomach, elevating up and down with the Ogre's every breath.

Across the campfire, Vee sat upon a large boulder, sharpening her stone daggers while casting a pensive gaze into the flames.

Arden stared at her in thought. He reached over to his satchel to retrieve something but paused to glimpse at Buffoh's makeshift tent of moth-eaten quilts. The drapes of its entrance had been left wide open. The boy bit his lip in contemplation, then quietly arose from his seat to see if the Leptoid was still awake. As he began to take a hesitant peek into the tent, a voice barked out.

"Ay! What are ya doin'?" Buffoh shouted.

Arden froze upon the repulsive sight before him.

There sat Buffoh, rubbing a thick yellow slime all over his feet and legs, like lard across a pan.

"Ya can't just sneak up on somebody like that," the man snapped.

"I-I'm sorry," Arden said, quickly closing his eyes to erase the vision from his memory. "Um... what's happening here?"

Buffoh pressed the gunk into his open pores and between his toes.

"What does it look like?" he grumbled. "I'm wipin' this lupper slime on myself. I don't want any garter beetles suckin' the blood outta my feet. Those nasty things are all

up and down these woods. I could do without 'em crawlin'
up in my business. Ya get me?"

"Alright then," Arden said, feeling
a tad queasy. "Sorry for both-
ering you."

Shuddering his nausea
away, the boy turned from
the scene, headed back outside, and abruptly closed the
drapes to the tent.

"What was that?" Vee
asked from across the
campfire, sheathing her
newly-honed daggers.

"A mistake," Arden said as
he walked over to the girl and
sat beside her on the boulder.

"So," he whispered, glancing
back toward Buffoh's tent.
"There's something I've been meaning to return to you but
I didn't want Buffoh to see."

Vee looked at him curiously.

The boy reached into his satchel, making sure the Leptoid hadn't been watching from afar. He pulled out a small
object and quietly placed it into the girl's palm. "I figured
you'd want this back."

Vee slowly opened her fist to see the amber necklace
she had traded with Buffoh.

"How did you—" she began.

"I swiped it from him while he was asleep in the tunnel
last night," Arden confessed. "I wanted to give it to you earlier, but Buffoh was always around, so..."

A shimmer gleamed in Vee's eyes as she held the necklace in her hand.

"Thank you," she whispered, wrapping the pendant around her neck and clutching its stone charm tightly.

Arden smirked. He hadn't stolen anything in weeks, and normally, he'd have gotten a thrill from such an act, but this time, it was different. Something about returning this cherished belonging to its owner just seemed right. Who knew that "un-stealing" something could feel just as rewarding?

"Hey, what happened to your blisters?" Vee asked, looking at the boy's exposed shins. "Didn't you get burned by that cave slime too?"

Arden glanced down to find his wounds had shrunken to mere blemishes.

"I *did*," he said.

"You weren't kidding about being a fast healer."

Arden shrugged. "Speaking of wounds, did you use that ferry tongue on your leg?"

"Oh," Vee said, shifting focus to her bandages. "Yes, actually." She gently began to untie the fabric straps concealing the injury.

The fire's warm glow illuminated her wound, and Arden could see it clearly now. To no surprise, the ferry tongue had worked wonders. The gash had nearly sealed shut, and the swelling had almost vanished.

"Wow!" Vee marveled. "This healed pretty well. Honestly, I didn't feel much pain after I used those leaves."

"See?" Arden asked. "I told you it would work."

He studied the injury some more, noticing the cut was healing in a perfectly clean line. It was certainly odd, especially for a scrape from a shrub, as the girl had claimed.

"It works on all kinds of injuries... actually," the boy added.

Vee's gentle smile fell flat, her curiosity piqued.

Arden gave a critical stare. "That wasn't from a thorn bush, was it?"

The girl slowly covered her wound. "What are you talking about?"

Arden let out a sigh. "Vee, I've lived in the woods long enough to recognize a scrape from a thorn bush. That gash on your leg—it's from a blade. Someone did this to you on purpose, didn't they?"

Vee shuffled uncomfortably.

"Why would you assume something like that?" she asked.

"Come on," the boy said, his voice insistent. "A mysterious wound that you tried to hide the truth about. Your lack of direction on how to get to Haroon. And that smoke we saw earlier—you seemed pretty nervous during all of that. Afraid, even."

"No, that's not—" Vee started.

Arden shook his head. "You're running from someone."

Vee's eyes grew glassy, and she turned away from the boy.

Arden quickly recoiled. He must have crossed a line, delving into such personal matters.

"I'm sorry," he said in a gentler tone. "Maybe this wasn't the right time to ask... but I wanted to know because I'm—"

"No. You're right—about all of it," Vee said, her voice bitter and full of regret. "I'm being hunted."

"Why?"

"Because I'm a fool, Arden," the girl said. She took a deep

breath. "Years ago, my parents' lives were taken by someone truly terrible. Since then, all I've wanted is to bring my family justice—to get revenge."

She turned back around with fire in her watering eyes. "Two days ago, I finally tried to avenge my parents' deaths—to face their killer head-on—but I froze, like the coward I am. A single moment of weakness nearly cost me my life, and in return, I was left with this cut on my leg—a reminder of how lucky I am to have escaped."

Arden remained silent, seeing the similarities between Vee's situation and his own—they were *both* being followed. He considered telling her the truth about his current dilemma. Then again, if he confessed, he'd have to explain why he was being followed by a hooded stranger and an Or'Ackin sorceress, which would surely lead to discussions of magic. And who's to say this girl would even believe him anyway? Besides, he certainly wasn't ready to tell her about the stone in his chest. There'd always be an opportunity to explain things later when he felt ready.

Being mindful, he finally answered, "I'm sorry about your parents."

"It doesn't matter anymore," Vee replied somberly. "What matters now is that I'm being followed by someone dangerous. I've only been able to tell their location from that campfire we saw, but it's been getting closer with every sunset. Reuniting with my sister is the only choice left for me. I have to reach Haroon and get as far away from these woods as I can, or else I'll end up..."

The girl hesitated, briefly placing her head between her hands before saying, "Arden, I want you to know I never intended to put anyone else's life in peril. So if you want me to leave, I'd understand."

Arden rubbed his chin in thought, then said, "If you

leave, you may never get another chance for your freedom. I can't have that on my conscience, especially knowing that you're in danger. If journeying north with us can help you escape, then I think you should stay. Of course, it's up to you, though. I'm not like Buffoh. I won't pressure you into making a decision. Honestly, I think he enjoys making people despise him."

A faint chuckle escaped Vee's lips, rising through the sorrow buried within her.

"So, what do you say?" Arden asked.

The girl tapped her thigh.

"Alright," she replied softly.

Arden smiled.

"Besides," Vee added, "as much as it pains me to say it, Buffoh may be right. We don't know what we're up against in that swamp. It might be wise to get all the help we can."

"True," Arden agreed. "Oh, and let's keep this conversation between us for now. I don't want the others panicking any more than they already are," he gestured toward Buffoh's tent with a thumb.

Vee nodded.

Chapter 15

Crossing the Bridge

Early that next morning, Arden woke up before the rest of the group and prepared breakfast. The boy had gone weeks without a decent meal, and Buffoh's cooking was somehow worse than Gord's.

He quietly grabbed a pan, a wooden spoon, and two carefully-wrapped eggs he'd found in a nest the day before. Amidst the campfire's ashy remnants, the young Elf placed fresh wood and kindled a new fire. As he took a seat, Arden pondered what style he wanted his eggs in.

Scrambled, he thought to himself, beginning to stir the yolks with the spoon.

The sizzling sound of breakfast brought fond memories of cooking with Gord in their little acorn cottage. The boy grinned at the thought.

Just then, the sound of fabric fluttered behind him as Buffoh came out of his tent. The man bellowed an enormous yawn, stretching his wide mouth into a cheerful smile.

"Ah!" he exclaimed, taking a deep breath of the humid morning air. However, his joyful expression quickly turned sour as a strong smell entered his nostrils. He covered his nose and leered at Arden's food. "What is *that*?"

The boy replied, "Breakfast. What else would it be?"

Buffoh hurried over, appearing even more repulsed. "We ain't got time for somethin' like this."

Before Arden could react, the Leptoid ripped the ceramic pan and wooden spoon from his hands and began banging them together as loudly as possible.

"Let's go, ya lazy folks. Wake up!" the man shouted.

Arden watched as his perfectly prepared eggs were pummeled into a rain of yellow soup. They sprayed into the air and fell at his feet, seeping into the dirt. Gone forever.

"Hey, I was going to eat that!" Arden yelled, but the clanging cookware drowned out his angry curses.

"Time is money, and we ain't got all day!" Buffoh continued.

The commotion startled Gord into a panic. He sprang to his enormous feet, seemingly ready for some horrible battle, but his gaze landed on the waist-high Leptoid with a ridiculous smirk on his face.

Mugz jumped up and began running around the campsite, barking frantically. She dashed around in circles, knocking into bags and grazing Vee's leg with her claws.

The girl winced from the sting and shot up, her eyes intense and half-open.

"What time is it?" she grumbled.

Buffoh slammed the pan even louder.

"Come on, people!" he yelled. "Ya ain't got a minute to lose if ya wanna get outta the swamp quickly. So, hurry ya butts up!"

Arden rushed over to the Leptoid and pried the pan from his hands. "Will you stop with the noise?"

As the clatter came to an abrupt halt, Mugz refrained from her barking.

"Just give us a moment! We'll get ready," the boy snapped.

"Fine!" Buffoh replied, stomping away to disassemble his tent. "Just make it quick."

Arden walked over to the campfire and doused its steady flames as the rest of the group prepared for the day ahead.

After their morning routine was finished and their campsite had been packed up, they set off once more, heading north through Feverwood Forest.

The hours passed steadily as they trekked deeper into the mossy woodland, their shoes crunching on an endless carpet of leaves and twigs. Eventually, the group had reached a massive veil of fog that engulfed the entire forest.

Through the haze, Arden could see the shadow of an enormous root, its many tendrils digging into the ground like fingers. Its gnarled frame stretched off into the haze beyond like a fallen tree.

"What is that?" he asked.

Buffoh paused, turning to the baffled travelers.

"That, folks, is the Bridge of Blackwater," he declared.

Arden and the others studied the imposing hunk of dry and rotted bark. It was a bridge indeed, but unlike any they'd seen before. Twisted and tangled, the dead root arched over a canyon up ahead and disappeared into the fog.

"Well, that doesn't look very promising," Arden remarked.

"You don't expect us to cross that old thing, do you?" Vee asked, shooting Buffoh a judgmental gaze.

"Well, how else do ya's plan on gettin' into the swamp there?" asked the Leptoid as he pointed toward the fog.

At that moment, a mysterious wind pushed the morning mist away, clearing the view beyond the tree bridge. Now, they could see its other end, clutching the opposite wall of the canyon like a hand.

Arden and his friends' eyes grew wide in amazement and terror. There, just past the bridge, sat Blackwater Swamp. They had finally made it.

Weeping willows spread from east to west like a festering wall. Each tree was wide enough to fit an entire house within its core and tall enough to hide a thirty-story tower. A low, green smog hovered just beneath each of their giant roots.

The place was vaster than Arden had imagined. A chill ran down the boy's back. He recalled Finn's tales of travelers who'd gotten eternally lost in this very swamp. It was certainly no place any *sane* person would enter. But still, somewhere deep within that ominous forest dwelled a witch with the answers he needed... hopefully.

Taking a deep breath, Arden walked closer to the edge of the canyon ahead. A thundering roar from below grew louder with the boy's every step. Curiously, he peeked over the side of the cliff. A ferocious river raged between Blackwater Swamp and Feverwood Forest, snaking through the land.

"Watch yaself, kid," Buffoh warned him. "That's probably the most dangerous river in all of Cynorrum. *Nobody* would make it outta that thing—alive, that is."

Arden kept his attention fixed on the menacing waters, noting the sharp rocks that peeked out like scattered teeth.

Buffoh dropped his pack with glee, clearly unfazed by the dangerous surroundings.

"Alright, kid. I've got ya armor in here," the man said,

handing Arden the bag. "Oh, and this map too," he finished, removing the rolled parchment tucked under his belt.

The boy was too focused on his thoughts of doom to respond.

"Kid, are ya gonna take this stuff or not?" Buffoh urged, shoving the bags into Arden's side.

The boy snapped out of his daze, wrapping his arms around the heavy pack.

"Good," Buffoh said. He went to a small, dead tree near the very edge of the cliff, snatched a large straw hat from his bags, and placed it on his head. Then, the Leptoid sat down and leaned against the tree to take a rest. "I'll be right here when ya's get out. Good luck, pal… and you too, lady."

The weary man shut his eyes and smiled with grace.

Arden took a moment to process the crazed Leptoid's words.

"When we get out?" he repeated in a whisper of disbelief.

Buffoh yawned, then replied through his sleepy grin, "Yep, when ya's get out."

"Wait, what?" the boy asked. "You said you'd take us through the swamp. That's why we came all this way."

The old Leptoid lifted the brim of his hat, looking at the confused Elf standing before him.

"No way, kid," he said. "I ain't goin' in there."

Arden turned to his father and Vee in astonishment to gauge their reactions.

Gord had dropped his belongings to the ground in complete shock.

Vee's face blazed with fury.

"Ay, don't get mad at me," Buffoh said. "It ain't my fault ya's all heard me wrong."

"We didn't hear you wrong, Buffoh," Vee growled. "We know exactly what you said."

Arden threw the map and bag of armor to the ground. "You promised to take me through the swamp and guide Vee to Haroon. Those were your exact words!"

Buffoh's lips quivered.

"I don't think so, kid," he snapped. "How many times did I tell ya that I don't go through there anymore? The deal was to take ya's *to* the swamp, not *through* the swamp."

"So what? You were just going to send us into this place by ourselves?" Arden asked.

Buffoh glanced back and forth between the two travelers, then replied, "Hey, I got ya's here, gave ya a map and some armor—I did my part, and this is the thanks I get?"

"Thanks? You're out of your mind," Vee interjected. "We don't know how to get through the swamp. That's what *you're* for!"

"No, that's what the *map* is for, which I so nicely carried all this way."

"I can't believe this," Arden replied. "I gave you all of the money I had—every last chip—and you lied to us!"

Buffoh snarled, hopping up from the tree roots and throwing his straw hat into the rapids below.

"Ay, I'm a lot of things, pal, but I ain't no liar!" he screamed, waving a finger in the boy's face.

Arden shoved the man's hand away. "This whole time, I thought I could trust you, but I was wrong. You're just a fraud. A cheap, scamming, no-good—"

A boomerang whizzed past Arden and Buffoh's heads, embedding itself in the tree behind them. The bark charred instantly, smoke billowing around the hot blade as it seared the wood.

The boy turned back toward the forest path from which the weapon had come.

In the gloom of the woods, a pair of white eyes set behind a rotted bird skull glared directly at him.

Arden's rage twisted into pure horror.

The Or'Ackin sorceress had found him. From atop her gringore, she leered upon the exposed travelers.

"It's her," Arden whispered shakily. "Run!"

Gord and Vee quickly sprinted to the tree bridge as Arden trailed behind.

Buffoh snatched the map and bag of armor from the ground, screaming as he too started across the giant root.

The Or'Ackin sorceress whipped her gringore, and the beast charged at them with great speed. In a swift movement, the woman pried her boomerang from the smoldering tree, then struck her whip once more.

The gringore leaped for the bridge, slamming down onto it with the weight of a dozen boulders.

Arden and his companions all stumbled in different directions as the root trembled and cracked. Even the sorceress nearly fell off the back of her beast from the rough landing.

Scrambling to their feet, the travelers bolted into the swamp as the Or'Ackin held onto her steed by its fur and pulled herself up to safety.

"Hurry, Buffoh," Arden yelled, glancing back at the Leptoid behind him. "Faster!"

The two of them plowed ahead, trying to catch up to Vee and Gord, but the sudden whistle of the sorceress's boomerang sang from behind.

"Get down!" the boy shouted.

Buffoh veered to the right as Arden dove left, narrowly avoiding the scorching weapon. Without a moment's rest, they sprang up and darted through the swamp in opposite directions.

Arden ran straight, dodging vines and jumping over roots until he entered an area filled with thick bushes. Spotting a denser shrub, the boy dove into it, wincing as the branches scratched his skin.

The pounding footsteps grew louder.

Arden pressed himself deep into the foliage, carefully moving branches and leaves to fill any spaces he might be seen through. The boy stayed as still as he could, holding a hand over his mouth to mute his heavy breathing. Through a gap in the bush, he watched as the dark creature slowed its pace to a steady crawl. His heart raced even faster, each beat echoing in his ears as he willed himself to remain calm.

The gringore began to sniff the air, its nostrils flaring and beady black eyes scanning the area. As the creature began to pass by the bush, Arden's eyes drifted upward from the gringore's balding forehead to the rider atop its hunched back.

Now, closer to the sorceress than ever before, Arden noticed that the Or'Ackin wasn't a bird person at all. Her skull-like face was only a mask, for beneath its bony frame, he could distinguish the woman's pale blue skin.

With her wild, gray hair flowing in the wind, the sorceress called out in a raspy voice, "I know you're here, Elf. You can't keep yourself from me forever. I have seen your mind. I have seen your very soul, and it shall be mine."

The Or'Ackin halted her mount and turned to stare upon the wall of bushes to her left. Though it appeared she couldn't see the boy, Arden felt as though she could sense his presence. A wicked grin stretched across the woman's lips. Her eyes shut tight, then flew open wide and began to glow brightly.

"Son... My son, where are you?" she whispered in a dozen soothing voices.

The Or'Ackin's lips remained motionless, but the space around her eyes began to ripple and pulsate like waves through the air.

Arden locked onto the hypnotizing sight and his surroundings faded into darkness. He suddenly felt as though he were being pulled through a deep and endless tunnel. The boy tried to resist the sorceress's soul-charming, but her enchanting tones clouded his thoughts, keeping him in the trance.

A force began to pull at his mind, and nothing seemed to matter but her motherly calls.

"Come to me. Follow your family," she whispered. "I'll tell you everything. Don't you want to know where you come from? Who you truly are?"

Without control, Arden took a firm step forward, snapping a branch beneath his foot.

As the sound resonated into the woods, the sorceress's eyes dimmed, and her gaze swung to Arden's exact location.

"There you are," she hissed.

Barbarically, the Or'Ackin whipped her gringore, and a deep roar bellowed from its maw as they barreled for the shrub.

In an instant, Arden was released from the trance, and the sights of the forest came into view once more. Summoning his strength, the boy stumbled out into the clearing as the gringore crashed into the bush.

Terrified, Arden bolted deeper into the swamp, weaving through the trees to keep his path unpredictable. The sorceress and her mount struggled to keep up with him, quickly falling behind as he veered further west.

Branches slapped against the boy's face, and thorns snagged his clothes, but he pressed on, determined to escape.

Eventually, the gringore's roars grew fainter and were replaced by the guttural hum of the forest. Arden slowed his pace, casting a cautious glance over his shoulder. Seeing no sign of the sorceress or her beast, he allowed himself a moment of relief. He stumbled forward a few more steps before collapsing onto the swamp floor.

It seemed he had eluded the Or'Ackin for now, but how long would that last? The boy remembered his father and friends were still out there... somewhere. What if the sorceress found them next?

With no time to waste, Arden stood up and surveyed the area. The beetle-like hum of the swamp filled the humid air, and the sun refused to cast its rays into the thickets. The only light that remained was the subtle glow of the green fog hovering above the ground.

"Gord! Vee! Hello?" the boy yelled in a whisper.

There was no reply. Arden was utterly alone in a perilous swamp with no guide, no friends, and no map.

CHAPTER 16

THE LIVING SWAMP

As Arden searched for his friends and family, Gord played a few notes from his flute, hoping his son would hear the familiar tune. Hours had passed since they were chased into the swamp, and the boy was still nowhere to be found.

"Arden! Arden!" Vee shouted, her voice echoing through the dark.

"Kid, where are ya?" Buffoh yelled.

While the worried travelers continued their cries, Mugz resorted to her powerful sense of smell, attempting to catch the boy's scent. Sadly, the overwhelming aromas of the swamp hindered even *her* skills. The stench of mold infested every black puddle, and the pungent odor of tree sap soaked the dirt. Mugz could barely smell *herself*, let alone track Arden down.

"Grr! It's no use," Buffoh groaned, glaring at the mugget. "That furball hasn't picked up a single trace of the kid yet. He's probably hours away by now, or worse—captured by that bird lady."

"You don't know that," Vee said frankly as she trailed behind Mugz's erratic path.

"No! I don't," Buffoh agreed. "But I do know one thing: none of this makes any sense." The Leptoid shot a wary stare in Gord's direction and asked, "I mean, why was that woman after us, anyway?"

The Ogre froze in his tracks, nervous that Buffoh might detect his unease. Even though Gord couldn't speak, he made sure to remain visibly calm so as not to appear suspicious. He simply shrugged his shoulders, dismissing the question.

"I guess it doesn't matter," Buffoh mumbled, shifting his attention back to the ominous trees. "The point is that it ain't safe for us out here. We could be searchin' for weeks."

Gord's concerns grew deeper as the group trekked onward. They should have at least found some sort of trail by now. Perhaps it was time to take matters into his own hands. Clearly, Mugz wasn't having any luck tracking the boy's scent. So, discreetly, Gord placed her on his shoulder and set off in a new direction.

"Ay!" Buffoh yelled. "Where do ya think ya goin'? Ya can't just walk out into the swamp like that—" The Leptoid quickly fell silent, twisting his arms into a firm knot. "Oh, I get it! Ya plannin' on leavin' us, huh?"

Gord marched forward, ignoring the man's accusations.

"I wouldn't be too quick to do that," Buffoh continued, a devious smirk set across his face. "Ya seem to be forgettin' that I'm the only one here with a map."

Gord made a dead stop. He turned his head around to the old toad with a stare that could melt stone.

"Mm-hm, that's right," Buffoh teased.

"I thought you lost that in the rapids," Vee replied.

"Nope," Buffoh said, pulling the map from his bags. "And now, since the furball can't get the kid's scent, a *proper* guide can take care of it. Ya welcome."

Gord angrily stomped back over to Buffoh, landing right at his feet.

"Good!" the Leptoid said sternly. "Now, onto business. We need to be smart about this before we go any further."

The old toad rummaged inside the bag he'd saved from

the rapids, retrieving some old cloth scraps. Though tattered and stained, he secured each one over his feet and fastened them with a string. Then, he gathered some oven mitts from his pack. Their once-blue fabric was caked with all kinds of dark sauces and gook, but the man slipped them over his dirty hands regardless.

"What are you doing?" Vee asked impatiently, tapping her foot.

"Puttin' armor on! What else?" Buffoh asked, securing the mitts. "The swamp is always watchin'... I mean it. This whole place is alive. It's readin' us right now. Feedin' on our fears, our nightmares, and who knows what else."

Vee rolled her eyes.

The Leptoid made one final shuffle through the over-stuffed bag before lugging out a ceramic pot. Its handles were chipped and scratched from years of use. Flipping the muck-covered thing upside down, the man dropped it on his head like a helmet.

"That's not how you use that," Vee muttered under her breath.

"Alright! I get it!" Buffoh mocked, adjusting his armor. "Sheesh! I swear, you and that kid are like the same person." The stubborn Leptoid consulted his map and surveyed their course before placing it back into his pocket. "I think that bird woman chased the kid west. So, let's start that way and get—"

The old toad gasped with fear, freezing in his tracks.

"Nobody move a muscle," he whispered, lips half closed as he tried to remain still.

Gord and Vee curiously squinted ahead at what had caught the Leptoid's attention. A small creature with no visible arms, spindly duck legs, and a clam-shaped body gazed back at them from a distance. The little beast was peculiar, but it seemed oddly fitting for their bizarre surroundings. Its pea-sized eyes were hard to discern amongst its bubbly skin, and its lower jaw jutted outward, revealing an assortment of teeth, both large and small.

Mugz began to emit a low growl, but Gord gently patted her head, trying to keep the mugget calm.

"What's that?" Vee asked.

Buffoh swiftly covered the girl's mouth with his grimy oven mitts.

"Sh! What's wrong with ya?" he hissed, turning to face her. "Don't ya know crogs get easily startled?"

Vee shoved the Leptoid's repulsive gloves away, spitting in disgust. "Oh, calm down. I mean, look at how ridiculous that thing is. How much danger could we possibly be in?"

"Ridiculous?" Buffoh asked with a nervous chuckle. "That *thing's* got poisonous skin! If ya don't take the right precautions, it's gonna—"

Suddenly, the crog began flailing its body forward in an awkward but terrifying display, squawking out obnoxious quacks.

Buffoh screamed, leaping onto Gord's round stomach for protection.

The crog jumped into the air and flung its weird body toward them, surprising Vee with its ability to lift its own weight.

CRUNCH!

A massive plant swooped out of the trees and chomped down onto the riled crog with a single bite.

Gord, Vee, and Buffoh stood with mouths agape as the carnivorous flower gave a loud gulp and retreated into the trees.

A moment of complete silence passed among the group.

"Uh, like I said," Buffoh stammered, climbing down off Gord's belly, "we gotta go west."

"Are you out of your mind?" Vee asked. "You want us to go in the direction that duck thing just came from?"

"Hey!" Buffoh barked. "We've gotta go that way if we're gonna find the kid, and ya's *do* wanna find him, right?"

Vee sighed, glancing up at Gord. The Ogre stared back at her anxiously.

"Yes," she said. "Just lead the way."

For the next few hours, they traveled deep into Blackwater, the fog turning thick and dense. Gord and Vee found themselves growing sick of the humid air and were constantly slapping bugs off their necks.

Buffoh, on the other hand, seemed to be doing just fine. Leptoids could adapt to this sort of environment, being toad people after all. A little humidity and a dozen flies here and there were the least of his problems. Every so often, he would whip out his tongue and snatch them up like they were free lunch.

Gord and Vee were frustrated by Buffoh's habits, but it wasn't the bug-eating that got to them—it was the man's sluggish pace.

Time seemed to move twice as slow, and Gord noticed Vee observing the swamp with a sharp eye. The girl abruptly stopped in her tracks and glared at their Leptoid guide.

"Hold on a minute. I remember these trees. We're going in circles, Buffoh!" she growled. "I bet you don't even know where we are, do you?"

Buffoh came to a halt and turned to the irate girl.

"Eh, you don't know what ya talkin' about. Of course, I know where we are," the Leptoid said.

"Oh really? Show me on the map then," Vee snapped.

"We're uh… right here, see?" he asked, pointing to a random area on the map and quickly pulling it away.

"What? Where? Let me see that again," Vee demanded, trying to snatch the scroll from the Leptoid's clammy hands.

"No! This is my map. I'm the only one who's gonna be readin' it," Buffoh said, pressing it firmly against his chest.

"You know what? Give me the map!" Vee shouted, lunging at the old toad.

"No! It's mine!" Buffoh screamed. "Find ya own map!"

Gord watched them brawl for the lousy piece of paper, unable to tolerate the bickering any longer. He walked over, threw his arm between them, and plucked the scroll from the Leptoid's grip with ease.

"Thank you!" Vee said, wiping her brow as Gord handed her the page.

Buffoh cursed under his breath.

"Now, let's see where we *really* are," Vee said.

Just before the girl could open the crinkly map, a long and slimy tongue snatched it from her grasp.

Buffoh peeled the scroll out of his mouth and held it high behind his head.

"Listen!" he shouted as he pulled the large scissor leg from his belt and held it defensively. "No one else uses this map except me. Ya got that?!"

Suddenly, two massive vines flew down from the branches above, swiped the items from Buffoh's hands, and disappeared back into the treetops.

The travelers stared up at the willows for a moment, processing.

"That's it. I'm goin' home," Buffoh said in a rather calm tone as he removed the cooking pot from his head.

Vee huffed.

"You can't go home now," she protested. "We had a deal!"

"Alright, let me tell ya somethin'," Buffoh replied. "A: not my problem. And B: I didn't sign up for this crap! As I recall, *you* wanted to do it all yaself. So enjoy, 'cause I'm done!"

The aggravated Leptoid began marching away into the unknown woods.

"Whatever then! I'll figure it out on my own," Vee said.

She too stomped off, but in the opposite direction.

Buffoh chuckled sarcastically, scaring away the flies near his face. He turned to glance at the enraged girl once more. "Ha! Ya ain't gonna last another minute—"

The man abruptly froze, and the tiny hairs on his head sprang upward.

"Stop!" he screamed.

Buffoh ran straight for Vee, jumping out in front of the girl to block her path.

"Don't step on that!" he said in a panic, sprawling his limbs out for maximum coverage.

Vee scoffed, halting in her tracks.

"What now?" she asked, peering over Buffoh's shoulder to the ground behind him.

Gord peeked around to catch a glimpse. Near Buffoh's heels was a small, flesh-colored grub wriggling up from the muddy grass. A thin fuzz coated its shiny skin, and an abundance of sharp red tentacles protruded from its eyeless head.

"Are you kidding me, Buffoh?" Vee asked. "A worm?"

"That ain't no worm!" the Leptoid said shakily. "It's a spiddle root. If ya step on it, this whole place is gonna go berserk. These trees will start movin' with a mind of their own. The ground's gonna ripple like waves. We'll be dead in no time!"

"Oh, give it a rest already, toad," Vee barked. "Can't you see we're done with your insane superstitions and constant worrying? 'Don't step on this. Don't touch that.' Well, I'm sick of it. I'm done taking orders from you. So, just stay out of my way!"

The girl shoved the Leptoid aside and stomped on the spiddle root's head with spite.

"No!" Buffoh shouted, gazing at the mangled root.

Vee continued ahead with satisfaction, seemingly unfazed.

"See? I told you," she said arrogantly. "Just another one of your ridiculous—"

A loud and terrible moan bellowed from the swamp, booming beneath their feet and vibrating through the trees. The nearby animals fled the scene, leaving the area devoid of life.

Vee glanced back at the helpless root as it writhed in pain.

In a flash, the little plant sucked itself back into the dirt, sending a small ripple through the mud. More ripples soon followed, quickly growing in size and number.

"I told ya not to step on it!" Buffoh screamed as he latched onto a boulder for safety.

Soon, the ground began to shift, waving like water in a raging sea. The once-solid ground now roiled and bucked, its movements unpredictable and violent. Trees that had stood firmly for ages now swayed perilously, their massive roots writhing like giant tentacles.

Gord frantically looked around, searching for something stable amid the chaos. In the distance, he managed to spot a rotted stump, stubbornly unmoved by the quaking. Without hesitation, the Ogre clumsily hopped toward it, hugging the trunk tightly as Mugz clung to his shoulder.

Hills continued to form, then sink away. Plants and rocks rolled in every direction. Nearby puddles, already filled to the brim, began to overflow, sending torrents of mud and grime.

Gord watched as Vee clawed at anything she could, but each wave of the shifting swamp sent her tumbling farther away. She attempted to keep her footing, but a massive vine swung down and slammed her to the ground. Unconscious, she drifted with the flowing land.

Gord wanted to make his way over to the girl, but the ground heaved violently beneath him, making it impossible to move. All he could do was cling to the stump, helpless.

Vee gasped for air as her eyes fluttered open. Expecting to still be drifting with the swamp floor, she was surprised to find that the terrain had finally settled.

The swamp had changed quite dramatically. No people. Not a single creature in sight. Only an empty expanse of unfamiliar trees. Even the murky fog that once hovered over the dirt had mysteriously vanished. The eerie stillness sent a shiver down her back.

Had she been asleep for hours or days?

The girl scanned her surroundings, searching for any sign of her fellow travelers.

"Gord! Buffoh!" she cried out, but the sound of her own yelling ached within her ears. The girl placed a hand on her head, wincing at the pain. For a moment, the darkness behind her eyelids was soothing, but something bright and orange began to shine through.

Vee peeked out, squinting at the forest path ahead.

In the distance was a flickering light, like that of a torch. It moved about aimlessly as if searching for something.

"Buffoh! Gord!" she shouted again, her heart beginning to race with glee, knowing her friends were close. "I'm over here!"

The fluttering ball of fire stopped abruptly, then jolted forward in her direction.

Vee could feel its heat, warming her face from afar. Her eyes widened in excitement, but as the gleaming object drew near, her hopefulness was quickly snuffed out by a terrible realization.

This was no torch approaching but a man whose body was engulfed in flames. Red smoke poured from the cracks between his molten skin, and his empty eyes glowed with fury as he charged for her.

Vee's stomach turned, and a rush of adrenaline coursed through her veins. She jumped to her feet and ran off toward a cluster of trees out of the pursuer's sight. Choosing carefully, she hid behind one of the timbers and held her breath, waiting for the man to pass.

As the fiery brute arrived, his footsteps slowed and he began to inspect the area with a confident stride.

In a calm but menacing tone, he called out, "Did you truly believe you could run from me?"

Vee could hear his scorching hand brush against each tree, setting them ablaze, one by one.

"You're just like them. Your family," he hissed, circling the area. "Weak—A spineless coward!"

Vee closed her eyes tightly as his voice grew near, wishing it would all end.

Now, only a single tree remained unignited by his flames: hers. The man paused, staring at it with a wicked grin. The fires of his body intensified, burning even brighter than before.

"I should have killed you when I had the chance," he yelled, clutching the timber with a blazing grip.

Vee rolled forward, barely dodging the flames as the final tree was set alight. A violent wall of fire rose from the ground, encircling her from all sides. A bitter smoke filled the air, and she held her chest in agony.

From beyond the edge of the inferno, the man's charred figure emerged, his body growing larger with each step.

"You'll never avenge anyone!" he roared, lifting his mighty fist above the girl. "By my hand, you will die here! This forest shall be your tomb!"

His arm swung down.

Vee squeezed her eyes shut, anticipating the intensity of his flames, but instead felt a clammy hand grab her shoulder.

An old and croaky voice cut through the high-pitched whine of the burning trees.

"Snap out of it, kid! Wake up!"

Vee hesitantly peeked out.

Squatting before her was a familiar Leptoid, his clothes spotted with mud and twigs.

"It's alright! See?" Buffoh said, holding a hand out toward Gord and Mugz behind him, their faces grave with concern.

"W-what? Where's the fire?" the girl stuttered, her voice trembling. "He set everything on fire!"

"Who? There's nobody else around," Buffoh reassured her. "It's just us!"

Vee's racing heart began to ease. No trees were set ablaze, no fiery man was trying to pummel her, and the ominous green fog over the ground had finally returned.

"Was that a dream?" she asked shakily.

"Yeah, and it happened to us too," Buffoh said. "The swamp does that sorta thing when ya step on those nasty spiddle roots. Why do ya think I didn't want to come back here? This place is an absolute nightmare."

A blush crept across Vee's face.

Gord walked over and offered his hand, carefully lifting her from the ground. He tore a small patch from his tattered shirt and handed it to the girl.

Vee hesitated, eyeing the cloth in confusion.

Gord pretended to wipe the sweat from his face with it, then pointed to her forehead.

"Oh," she said, looking upward as she dabbed her soaked brow.

His kind eyes lingered on her.

Vee cracked a smirk, looking down at the cloth. "Thanks," she said. "So, what happened to you guys?"

"Well, I got chased by a yip," Buffoh replied, shivering at the memory. "It was terrible. But luckily, the furball over here woke me up and led me to the Ogre just a few minutes before we found ya."

Mugz chirped with glee.

"I guess the swamp can't play its tricks on animals," Buffoh continued.

"I suppose not," Vee said. "Listen, we can't stay here forever. We have to find Arden before he steps on one of those spiddle roots... if he hasn't already."

Gord and Buffoh nodded.

Mugz hopped off the Ogre's shoulder and began sniffing around.

"Right. We ain't got time to lose," Buffoh said, reaching for his belt. "Now, where did I put that map?"

"It's gone, remember?" Vee asked. "The vines took it."

"Damn! I forgot about that," the Leptoid said, snapping his fingers.

Mugz began to bark, skittering around a pile of leaves in excitement. The lack of wildlife from the swamp's shifting had given the mugget the ability to track again. She aimed her body westward, signaling for everyone to follow.

Gord's eyes lit up with joy as Mugz began to scurry away.

"Come on!" Vee exclaimed. "She's found Arden's trail!"

Chapter 17

Whispers from the Willow

"Gord! Vee! Where are you?" Arden shouted, tightly holding the gribic's eye Buffoh had given him for luck.

Hours had passed since the boy first began his search. At this point, he cared less about finding the witch and more about reuniting with his friends and family.

"Is anyone there?!" Arden cried out, but his voice just seemed to echo back at him. He had retraced his steps countless times, but the winding paths had all begun to look the same.

The boy gazed back down at the revolting gribic's eye in his hand, studying the foggy pupil that stared back at him tauntingly. What a foolish idea it was to believe that this disgusting thing could bring any amount of luck.

"Oh, what am I thinking?" he growled, his frustration swelling. "I'm never going to find them in this forsaken place—not without a map or a guide, and especially not with *this* damn thing!"

Arden clenched the reptilian organ between his fingers, raised his arm, and chucked it as far as he could. He watched as it bounced off the roots of a nearby tree and rolled into the darkness of the swamp ahead. The boy stood, panting heavily with rage.

He began heading in a new direction, but Buffoh's warning suddenly rang through his mind, "Drop the eye, and you'll have runny bowels for a month—a whole month."

Arden groaned.

Watch that be the one thing that old toad was actually right about, he thought.

Beginning an angered search, the boy felt his way through the shadows, fumbling over muddy branches and moss-covered rocks. Glancing further off, he finally saw the eye lying face down in the dirt by a wall of dangling vines.

Arden rushed over and grabbed the slippery object from the mud. Its fresh layer of slime nearly made him gag, but he brushed off the filth just in case.

As the boy arose, a faint glow shone onto his face from behind the drapery of the vine wall. Its steady radiance warmed his damp cheeks like a ray of daylight. But that was impossible. It should've nearly been nighttime by now. Maybe it was a torch. No, it was far too warm—too bright to have been that. But it could've been a campfire. Perhaps his friends were just on the other side.

A muffled noise began to tremble from beyond the shimmering light. The distant whispers grew louder and he could hear someone talking from behind the foliage.

Arden quickly straightened his pose. He glanced once more at the gribic's eye in his palm, feeling as though its luck had found him after all. Quickly placing the eye back into his satchel, he pushed the vines aside and stepped into the brightness.

"Buffoh? Vee? Is that you?!" he shouted.

Adjusting to the blinding rays, the boy's hopefulness seemed to dissolve away as he regained focus. There were no friends to greet him, nor was there a campfire of any sort. Instead, Arden was now gazing upon hundreds of strange glowing orbs floating about like miniature suns.

In this wide space, canopied by the towering thickets, the yellow orbs seemed to drift all around, illuminating the area. At its center stood a large, gnarled tree.

Arden marveled at the sight, feeling as though he had just stepped into another world. From afar, he observed the dead tree some more, noticing the moss-covered bark swirling up its trunk. Atop its crooked branches rested dozens of brown vines, dangling like hair. And then, there were its two orange eyes that blazed beside its jagged beak.

Wait! the boy thought. *A twisted body? Hair like vines?*

Finn's tale of the swamp witch replayed in his head. But this tree was no creature. It was just a house. Arden could see the resemblance now: the round, candle-lit windows staring back at all who gazed upon them and the rotting door under its beak-like gable.

A fragrance similar to cinnamon rode on the soft breeze as a trail of smoke billowed from the cottage's branch chimney.

Could this have been the swamp witch's domain?

Hesitantly, Arden approached the cobblestone steps of the cottage. It was evident from their dirt-covered surfaces that the stones hadn't felt the scamper of a creature, nor the footsteps of a traveler, in ages.

The boy cautiously walked up to the splintered door, lifting his hand to knock, but his confidence fell flat. He paused, worrying who, or what, might be lurking inside the eerie dwelling. Could it really be a beast of pure disgust, like Finn said? A wicked fiend with three eyes and sharp teeth?

Arden peeked his head toward the window to get a better view, but the glass was covered in years of dust. Only the soft glow of a fireplace could be seen through the pane. He took a deep breath and raised his knuckles.

"Hello? Is anyone home?" he asked, knocking three times.

For a good while, only silence answered him.

Arden sighed, growing impatient as doubt began to bubble in his stomach. He knocked once more, but still, there was no response.

Would he ever get the answers he sought, or have this stone removed from his chest? This entire journey felt like a waste. Frankly, he wasn't even sure if the witch really lived here, but he certainly couldn't break in just to find out. An empty pit began to form in his core, realizing he'd put himself and his family in danger for nothing. And what was more important anyway: trying to find some witch or reuniting with them?

Arden tried to swallow the disappointment as he walked back down the steps.

Just then, the sound of shattering glass echoed from within the tree cottage.

As the boy pivoted to look, a shadow whipped past the left window.

Arden rushed to the door, eagerly knocking once more.

"Come back! I know someone's in there!" he yelled.

A knot in the door opened up, and a large black eye filled its emptiness.

Arden jumped back, stumbling down the rocky steps.

The eye leered at the boy, scanning him from head to toe. Then, a small voice muttered from behind the door, "G-go away. You're not welcome here."

"Wait!" Arden said with haste. "There's someone I need to see—The Witch of Blackwater Swamp. I was told she lives here."

"No—no, you're mistaken," the voice snapped. "There are no witches here, so just go!"

The stranger's eye disappeared, and the small knot slammed shut, sealing the hole in the door.

Arden flinched at the sound.

"I can't be mistaken," he said desperately. "This *has* to be the witch's house. I just know it! Please—I need your help... You're my last hope."

There was a tense pause.

Arden's hands grew clammy as he waited for a response.

CLICK!

The door unlocked, creaking open to reveal a shadowy figure silhouetted by candlelight.

"Are you a hunter? A spy?" they asked.

"No," Arden replied, staring at the stranger with intrigue. "I'm neither."

A leathery-skinned foot, tipped with long curled nails, crept out into the light.

Arden backed away as a small, elderly woman with giant pointed ears stood before him.

She was as ancient-looking as the world around her. A moss shawl was draped over her bony frame, and messy curls spiraled behind her high shoulders. Upon her triangular face sat two eyes, one clenched shut and the other open, black as pitch.

She wasn't some terrifying creature of legend but a frail little Troll: beings long forgotten by most in Cynorrum.

"Well, child," the woman said with a sudden but kind smile, "Tell me... why have you traveled all this way to visit a witch like myself?"

Arden took a deep breath, pulling his collar down to the bottom of his scar.

"Because of this," he said, displaying the cloudy-blue stone half-submerged in his heart.

The witch's grin slowly flattened. She grunted under her breath, staring at the oddity. After a moment of contemplation, she spun around and gestured for the boy to follow her inside.

Could this woman really have the answers he'd been seeking his whole life?

Trembling with anticipation, he stepped up through the doorway, wondering if he'd leave this place the same person he once was.

As Arden walked inside, the front door seemed to close by itself behind him. Perhaps this *was* a house of magic, after all.

He gazed around the main room of the cottage. Dozens of trinkets were scattered about the floor, and random objects dangled on strings from the jagged ceiling. Potion bottles and jars cluttered every shelf. Piles of spell books were stacked against the walls. It was a mess, to say the least. Not even Buffoh's shop could hold a candle to the clutter of this place.

The witch, seemingly accustomed to her crowded living space, hobbled left toward a massive ceramic cauldron and mixed the slushy brown porridge inside.

"What is your name, Elf?" she asked.

The boy veered his focus back to her.

"Oh, it's Arden," he replied.

The old Troll bowed with pleasure. "Well, Arden, my child, I apologize for my skepticism before, but you must understand, I've had quite a few hunters come to my door-step in the past. But never has such a young fellow like yourself wandered into my neck of the swamp. Most folks that come through here are much older or much more ter-rifying. So, I must ask, wherever are you from, dear?"

"I'm from Noakwood Hollow," Arden said.

"Ah! The forests of Graveen. That's mighty far from here," said the witch. She moved away from the cauldron and placed a spidery hand on the boy's shoulder. "By the looks of you, I'd say you're starved as ever. Don't be shy. Please have a seat at my table. Perhaps I could offer you something to eat, yes? I'm making a scrumptious brew over here. It may be my finest yet."

The food did smell rather good, and Arden's stomach was rumbling out of control.

"Sure, why not?" he agreed.

The witch cackled with glee.

"I believe you'll find it quite tasty. It has some of that candied moss from Mandoril. Ooh! It's my favorite," she said, licking her lips.

Arden smirked and took a seat by the old table against the wall. It was lopsided and round, similar to the one he had back home. A familiar and comforting feeling rushed over the boy like he was about to have supper with his fam-ily again.

"Well, here you are," said the witch, filling up a bowl of porridge and placing it on the table. "Go on. Eat up!"

Arden analyzed the meal before him. Though mushy and soft, the sweet-smelling porridge seemed to glow with a golden hue, like roasted apples glazed with sugar. A low and gentle smoke trailed off its warm edges.

Arden dug his spoon into the bowl and took his first bite.

"Wow!" he exclaimed as an explosion of wondrous flavor instantly flooded his taste buds. "This is amazing."

He began throwing big spoonfuls of the stuff down his throat, and the old woman chuckled lightheartedly.

"Never doubt a granny's cooking, dear," she said, dusting off the adjacent chair and slumping into its firm seat. "Been doing it for a long time now."

Still stuffing his cheeks, Arden asked, "How long have you been making this?"

The old Troll leaned back, tapping her sharp chin. "Oh, well, let's see... Perhaps over two thousand years. It's hard to say, really."

Arden let out a loud cough as he attempted to swallow what remained in his mouth.

"Two thousand?!" he repeated. "You're way older than I thought—I mean—I'm sorry. That came out wrong," he said, his face beginning to blush. "Um, well, anyway... I can't imagine the stories you must have—the many people you've probably met."

The witch tilted her head downward, her giant nose practically reaching her chest.

"You might think so, child," she said somberly. "But live as long as I have, and all of those stories and faces begin to get a bit muddied. I've seen many come and go; my very people vanish into dust. And, in all the darkness and tragedy that has unfolded before my very eye, I must sadly admit that I've forgotten most things... even my own name."

Arden sat back in awe, unsure of what to say. He'd never imagined someone could grow so old that they'd forget their name.

"It's no matter," the witch continued, waving a hand. "I hardly wish to remember the past, anyway. The only things

I truly cherish anymore are my belongings and simple moments in life, like you and I at this table right here, sharing in sweet conversation."

Arden smiled, enjoying their tranquil moment. But then, a loud noise interrupted them.

The cauldron began to bubble out of control, and the witch rushed to tend to it. Arden watched as she stirred the pot, humming a merry tune.

He couldn't help but say, "You're not at all like I expected."

"Is that so?"

"Yes. You know, I've heard tales about this place and about you. Honestly, I thought I'd be meeting someone a little more—"

"Vile, dear?" asked the woman.

"No. Not that—"

"Wicked?" she pressed.

"No! Not that either—"

"What then? A hideous beast with three eyes and the body of a worm?" she snapped.

The hairs on Arden's neck stood straight up, and his pose stiffened. He never meant to offend her.

The old witch abruptly burst into laughter, her cackle bouncing around the walls.

"You don't have to flatter me, child," she said in a much sweeter tone. "People have made me out to be quite the character, haven't they? Time and again, I do get a good laugh from those stories. But truthfully, it still breaks my poor old heart. How could they say such terrible things without ever having known me?"

Arden remained silent, feeling pity for the old woman.

He even felt a bit guilty for having believed in such offensive rumors about her.

"Oh, enough about me," she continued, plucking the ladle from the cauldron and hanging it on a hook. "You're here to find out what lies in that chest of yours. Well, let's have another look, shall we?"

Arden suddenly remembered why he had come. Having been so caught up in their little chat, he'd almost forgotten.

"Oh, right," he said, pulling down his collar once more.

The witch's one good eye was deeply fixated on the glistening gem in his chest.

"Hm, very curious," she said before thrusting an ear against the stone as if listening for secrets.

"You wouldn't believe the trouble this thing has put me through," Arden said, trying to ease the awkward moment. "I ended up visiting a gemologist friend of mine—just to see if he could figure out what this thing was."

"A gemologist?" the witch repeated, still listening to the stone. "What did he tell you, dear?"

Arden shrugged. "He believed it to be some kind of old stone, maybe even an *ancient* one."

"Oh, it is indeed," replied the witch, leaning away from his scar. "As old as I, actually."

"So, it is true!" Arden said, shifting in his chair. "Well, can you tell me where it came from or why I have it? I need answers—anything! I've dragged my whole family into this mess and—Ow!"

The witch plucked a single hair from his head with a good yank. Then, she walked over to the cauldron, holding the hair over the billowing steam with a grim expression.

"What was that for?" Arden growled, rubbing his throbbing scalp.

"Clarity!" the witch whispered.

She gently released the hair from her fingers and it twirled down into the boiling pot.

POOF!

The contents of the cauldron swirled about. The once-calm smoke roared and thundered as a gust of wind blew out every candle in the cottage. An eerie darkness filled the room as the fire dwindled down.

The plucked hair singed within the pot, and the witch leaned in close. A thin stream of smoke whirled up from the hair, accompanied by the sinister chorus of a hundred ghostly whispers.

The Troll-woman shut her good eye and inhaled, filling her lungs as her head slowly waved back and forth. She let out a sudden gasp, and her blind eye flew wide open. The cauldron's water blazed bright green, casting a haunting glow on her face.

Arden watched in awe as the old witch spoke in an echoed and raspy voice,

"Embodiments of Life and Death,
Hailed, one from East and one from West.
In battle fierce, their bodies fell;
In stone, their souls remained to dwell.

But even after they'd depart,
A fate was sealed for both their hearts.
Though each was kept below the ground,
There was one lost, whilst other found.

The heart of Death lies buried deep,

Awoken from eternal sleep.
A creature lurks beyond the grave
And guards the heart no thief can save.

Beware this creature's breathless growl—
The cry of thousands in its howl.
Though just a shadow of itself,
This beast could kill the witless Elf.

A prophecy must be fulfilled:
That evil beast ought to be killed.
To find Death's heart, endure the gloom.
Look just beneath ancestors' tomb."

A blinding burst of light flashed out. In an instant, all of the smoke in the cottage was sucked back into the pot. The green glow dimmed as the cauldron's fire returned to a warm orange. The candles around the room had all sparked back up, their flames waving gently.

"Lovely!" said the witch in delight as her black eye reopened and her pale one sealed shut again.

Arden was the only thing left in that house that hadn't reverted to normal. His jaw remained agape.

Well, the witch sure did give him some answers, but nothing he could comprehend—just a cryptic riddle.

"I can't believe you got all that from one hair," the boy said, almost sarcastically. "But I still don't get it. What does that have to do with my stone?"

The elderly woman strolled away from the brew, shrugging off the prophecy. She collected all sorts of objects from around the crowded house: a few fish heads from a crate, a handful of worms from a cloudy jar, and even a smelly old sock. She gathered all the items into her long arms and tossed them into the bubbling porridge.

A puff of brown smoke coughed out from the cauldron. Its sweet scent of apples and spices quickly morphed into a terrible odor.

Arden winced at the smell but couldn't care less. All he wanted was some explanation of what had just transpired.

Two embodiments of life and death? Souls that remained? A beast to defeat? he wondered.

The witch continued making a loud ruckus as she collected more ingredients.

"Please!" Arden said, trying to refrain from interrupting the woman. "I don't understand. Can you give a clearer explanation?"

The witch snatched a black and purple mushroom from a cabinet, brought it close to her nose, and gave it a good whiff.

"No!" she said, tossing the wretched fungus over her shoulder.

"D-do you mean to me or the mushroom?" Arden asked.

The woman kept silent.

"Can you remove the stone?" the boy pleaded with despair in his voice.

The clatter of bottles and jars came to a halt, and the witch ceased adding items to the cauldron. Her expression grew serious as she walked over to the Elf with both hands on her heart.

"My dear boy, I fear that removing it whilst you're alive could be disastrous—maybe even fatal. You couldn't possibly want *that*," said the witch before searching the shelves above Arden's head. "Watch out, dear!"

The boy began to pick at his nails anxiously. Her words had shattered his hopes to pieces. Finn's theory was true; removing it *could* kill him.

"Well, what am I supposed to do then?" he muttered in defeat. "If you can't remove it, how am I supposed to be free of all of this chaos?" He paused, then said, "Gord was right. I never should have—"

"Whoopsie!" the witch exclaimed.

A leather pouch fell from the shelf above. The woman reached out and firmly slapped the bag against the table. A plume of red powder burst forth from the pouch, wafting toward Arden.

The boy gasped, lifting a hand to shield his eyes from the cloud, but the dust had already covered his face. He squinted through the pain, forcing a stream of tears down his cheeks.

As Arden tried to wipe away the powder, the witch grabbed ahold of his wrists and said, "Oh, you poor child. Don't rub—that'll only make it worse."

Careful to heed her warning, the boy stayed as still as he could, his arms hovering in place above the table.

"I'm truly sorry about that. You'll have to excuse these old fingers of mine—clumsy as a crog," the witch said with a chuckle. "Now, stay right here, dear—I'll get you cleaned up and ready in no time."

The woman hurried away into a dimly lit room behind the cauldron.

Arden sat there as an unbearable aching began to throb in his ears. The once pleasant taste of the witch's porridge had now warped into the putrid flavor of rancid meat. He drew his dizzy focus to the bowl on the table, hopeful that fixating on something stationary might ease his nausea.

As the cloudiness in his eyes cleared, Arden noticed something peculiar. Was his porridge... breathing? The sloppy mush seemed to move on its own, shifting around in the bowl as if awakening from slumber. Its golden hue aged into a sickly gray color.

Arden shoved the revolting dish away, forcing a veiny object to bob to the surface. It sloshed up and down, slowly rotating to reveal a bloodshot pupil.

Repulsed, the boy jumped out of his chair, knocking it to the floor.

"I have to go!" he said, stumbling to the front door.

Just before he reached it, a voice called out, "Where are you going, my child?"

The witch was suddenly back in the room.

Arden dared not look at her. He tried to lift his hands for the doorknob, but his limbs went numb.

"I g-go n-now," he attempted to say.

"Go?" the woman asked, glancing over at his half-eaten meal. "But you've hardly finished your food," she said, her voice turning shrill and sad.

Arden finally grasped the doorknob, but it rapidly locked itself. He swiveled back around toward the witch, and she grinned at him with glee, licking her lips. A heavy drool spilled from the corners of her mouth as the fires of the cauldron grew hotter.

"L-let me out!" he tried to yell, but exhaustion overtook him, and he tumbled backward, smacking against the door and collapsing to the ground.

The sickening spin in his head intensified. He gazed back at the witch. It seemed there were three of her now, each translucent apparition drawing closer as the surrounding room stretched further away.

"But don't you want to stay here with me?" she asked.

"N-no. No!"

The witch sighed. "Oh, but you do, Arden. I'll keep you safe. Keep that stone of yours safe. With me, my dear, no one will ever find it again. Give it to me, and you can be free from all the troubles it's caused you. You'd like that, wouldn't you?"

Arden couldn't fight it. A soft whisper escaped his mouth.

"Yes," his voice replied.

"That's it, dear! And you want to stay with me—forever. Say that, child. Won't you?"

Arden's face went blank as he lay on the floor. His heartbeat slowed to a mere thump.

"I want to stay with you... forever," he repeated, unwillingly.

The witch cackled with joy, raising her arms out wide. Slowly, dozens of sharp bones and sticks began to float into the air behind her, appearing from every crack and corner of the house.

As they circled the room, Arden began to feel a strange peace and closed his eyes.

The witch snapped her fingers, and the levitating objects froze, aiming themselves straight for the boy's head.

Suddenly, a voice thundered from outside. "Arden! Arden!"

The old Troll witch gasped, glaring out the window as another voice croaked, "Kid, where are ya?"

Arden's eyes flew open at the familiar calls.

"B-Buffoh? Vee?" he whispered.

His tranquility waned as another cry from Buffoh shook the cottage.

The old woman wailed in terror as her floating objects fell to the floor. "No! Don't listen to them!"

Arden twitched his fingers as the witch's spell weakened. His own thoughts found their way back into his head.

Move. Get up. Run!

Regaining his strength, he reached for a thick book nearby, clutched it tightly, and hurled it at the witch. Its pages fluttered like wings as it flew across the room and slammed into her stomach.

With a painful howl, she went crashing into the dining table, shattering it to pieces.

Though Arden's legs were still numb, he forced himself up, grabbed a handful of books, and headed for the windowsill. Only one thought consumed him now.

Get out.

Without hesitation, he shielded his face with the books and leaped for the window.

The witch raised her hand as she lay curled up on the ground. In an instant, the swarm of twigs and bones shot up from the floor toward Arden as he went crashing through the pane.

As the boy tumbled down a large root in front of the cottage, the speeding projectiles flew over his head and into the depths of the swamp.

The musty air flooded Arden's lungs, purging the poisonous powder from his body. For a moment, he rested, expecting to see his friends nearby, but they were nowhere in sight.

He scanned his surroundings. The glowing orbs that floated throughout the witch's domain dimmed one by one.

Her spell *was* breaking.

A spine-chilling screech roared from inside the house, and the witch burst out the front door, flying on a stick with great speed. She angled high into the air and banked right, circling the tree to find the boy.

Arden frantically attempted to gain his bearings. Though everything outside was much darker than before, he scampered to his feet and ran for the swamp.

His vision was still hazy and warped, making it hard to tell which direction he was facing.

"Come back! Come back!" cried the witch as she began to close in from behind.

Arden lunged forward, stamping over rocks and ducking under tree roots.

The witch's shrieks grew more distant the further he ran. Eventually, the only sound he could hear was the pounding of his own footsteps.

As Arden slowed down and hid behind a tree to catch his breath, Vee's voice echoed across the sky once more.

"Arden!" she yelled, her voice muffled and echoing as if she were somewhere off to his right.

The boy lit up with hope as he looked toward the direction of the call.

Out of nowhere, another loud sound whooshed above. The witch soared overhead on her gnarled branch, swerving between the treetops and hooking back around.

As the Troll plummeted straight for the boy, she reached out her sharp claws.

Arden held his ground, waiting for the right moment.

Just as the witch was about to reach him, he jumped out of the way.

The old woman's branch violently snapped in two against the tree and she went crashing into a mass of thorny bushes nearby.

Arden sprinted for Vee's voice, refusing to glance back.

Soon, he came upon a wide clearing devoid of trees. He skidded to an abrupt halt, arriving at the edge of a dark lake, barely able to tell it was there.

Across the water, he heard his friends' cries growing louder.

"Where is he?!" said Buffoh from someplace nearby, the water rippling with the sound of his voice.

Arden studied the opposite side of the pond. There in the distant reflection of the water was a faint yellow light, dancing across the surface like a burning torch. Squinting to get a better view, he could see the upside-down reflections of his friends, walking along the coast. The boy panned back up to the adjacent treeline but saw no sign of his fellow travelers.

Was he stuck in some sort of mirrored version of the swamp? A realm created by the witch herself?

Just then, the witch's screech pierced the forest.

Arden quickly looked back to see the woman charging for him on all fours.

"Gord! Buffoh! Vee! I'm here! I'm right here!" the boy shouted over the water, but his friends couldn't hear him.

The witch's roar drew close.

Arden held his breath, took a great leap, and dove head-first into the pond. As he entered, the weight of the water felt unusually heavy, as if he were at the bottom of the lake.

Now, the sounds of his friends' calls were even closer than before.

Arden opened his eyes to the sting of the murky waters.

The flame of a torch shined brightly from below... or was it above? Either way, the boy was running out of time and had nowhere else to go. Trying his best to save the air in his lungs, Arden swam toward the light.

Chapter 18

A Rapid Escape

Arden sprang up from the murky depths, gasping for air as he choked on dirty water. Slimy vines clung to his soaked clothes, drooping over his entire body from head to toe.

Suddenly, a croaking scream cut through the swamp, "Oh, no! This is it! It's happenin'! It's a yip!"

Between the seaweed draped over his hair, Arden saw Buffoh jump from the coast and onto a pile of rocks, hollering like a lunatic.

"That's no yip," Vee exclaimed. "It's Arden!"

As the boy removed the tangled vines from his head, Gord darted to the shore, and Mugz barked with excitement.

Buffoh lowered himself off the boulders.

"Oh, kid, it's just you," he said, trying to appear calm. "What are ya doin' in there?"

Still catching his breath, Arden investigated the surrounding waters. He expected the witch to yank him back down into the depths, but to his relief, nothing emerged. No bloodthirsty Trolls. No ravenous fish.

"I uh—accidentally dropped the gribic's eye you lent me, and it rolled into the lake," he said, thinking on his toes. "Then, I remembered you mentioning something about having runny bowels for a month."

Buffoh gasped, shaking his head nervously. "Did ya find it, at least?"

Arden peeked into his flooded satchel, and the gribic's

eye bobbed up, looking straight at him.

"Here you go," he said, tossing it back to Buffoh.

The Leptoid caught the slime-covered thing in his hands.

"Mother of muck, kid," he said under his breath, rubbing off the gunk. "Ya could've at least cleaned it first."

Arden pulled the stray bits of seaweed from his hair and asked, "So, what happened to all of you?"

The three companions exchanged glances of bewilderment.

"You wouldn't believe us if we told you," Vee admitted.

"I think you'd be surprised," Arden replied, trudging out of the lake to the muddied coast.

Vee gave a smile. "Good to have you back."

Gord rushed over to embrace his son. The Ogre's eyes welled up as he held the boy tightly.

Mugz weaved between Arden's ankles with glee.

"Uh-huh, yeah. Glad to have ya back, kid," Buffoh interjected, watching the emotional scene unfold before him. "And, now that we're all together again—why was that bird woman chasin' ya anyway?"

Caught off-guard, Arden released himself from Gord's arms and stammered, "Oh, sh-she's... I have no idea." The boy knew no one would buy such a terrible response, but the words seemed to fall from his mouth.

"Ya sure about that?" Buffoh asked with skepticism. "'Cause ya seemed to recognize her when she spotted us at the bridge."

"No, I didn't," Arden said with hesitation.

"Yeah, ya did. Ya even told us to run."

"Well, I—"

"Do ya know who she is?" the Leptoid questioned with scrutiny.

"I-I don't."

"I think ya do."

Arden looked to Gord for help, but the Ogre just shook his head nervously.

The boy swung to Buffoh quickly and said, "What I meant is that I don't *know* her, but I know *of* her."

"Great. So now we're gettin' somewhere. Who is she to *you*?"

"Oh, was she that old friend you were supposed to meet in the swamp?" Vee asked.

"No. No! She's—" Arden stammered.

"Friend in the swamp? Ya never told me about that," said Buffoh.

"I *did* tell you," the boy said. "When we were going through that tunnel the other day, Vee and I talked about it, but you were walking ahead of us—"

"I don't remember that," the Leptoid snapped. "And that wasn't part of our deal."

Vee gazed at Buffoh curiously. "But isn't that why Arden paid you to take him through the swamp in the first place?"

"Of course not, and do we need to go over this whole *to* the swamp or *through* the swamp thing again? I had no idea why the kid wanted to come out here. I was just lookin' to get paid."

"Well, he said he was meeting a friend," the girl replied, turning back to Arden. "You *are* meeting someone here, aren't you?"

All eyes were on Arden now. The boy had feared this moment. And sure, he suspected a time might come when pressing questions would arise, but he never imagined it happening all at once like this.

Arden sighed, gazing at his father with disappointment. A deep pain grew in the boy's chest as he came to terms with his only option. No more lies. He couldn't keep hiding from this, no matter how badly he wanted to.

Don't, Gord signed discreetly.

Arden answered him aloud, "I have to tell them."

"Tell us what, kid?" Buffoh asked as he crossed his arms.

Vee followed suit.

Arden took a deep breath, building up the courage to finally speak. "Look, there's something you don't know about me—something I didn't want to admit. But I can't keep this a secret any longer... It's time I told you the truth."

"We're listening," Vee said.

Gord grabbed Arden's shoulder, pulling him to the side. *Son, if you do this, there's no going back.*

"I know! I know," the boy said, waving a hand. "But I trust them."

Gord gave a deep stare but surrendered a nod.

The boy turned to his companions, then said, "I'm not really from Aramore. Gord and I live in Noakwood Hollow, just outside of it... alone. I've never even lived amongst other Elves before."

Arden paused, summoning the courage to continue.

"And I didn't come to the swamp to meet an old friend. The real reason I'm here is because... I was trying to find a witch."

Vee's brow steepened.

Buffoh gave a hearty laugh and said, "The Witch of Blackwater Swamp? Yeah, right, kid."

"Do you really expect us to believe that?" Vee asked.

"Yes, I'm serious. That's why I'm here," Arden replied.

The boy's friends squinted at one another, clearly unconvinced.

"Look, I know I haven't been honest, but I'm trying to be now—"

"So be honest then," Vee said bluntly.

"I am!" Arden replied, beginning to lose his temper.

"Witches ain't real, kid," Buffoh said. "I've been here a million times and never came across no witch. She's just a legend."

"Really?" Arden asked. "You, of all people—with all your superstitions—don't believe in witches?"

"Fine," Buffoh blurted out. "Let's say I did—which I don't—but let's say I did... then what business would ya even have visitin' someone like her, huh?"

"Because I needed her to remove this," Arden confessed, pulling down his collar to reveal the stone in his chest.

Vee and Buffoh stood in shock, their eyes wide open as they observed the oddity.

Gord watched his son with terror etched across his face.

"Well, that explains it," said Buffoh, breaking the awkward silence.

"What is that?" Vee asked with intrigue.

Arden blushed, tying up his collar.

"It's some kind of stone, from what I've been told," he said, shying away. "I don't know what its purpose is, but I've had it for as long as I can remember. It's the reason I came all this way. I needed to know if the witch could remove it."

"I mean, even if the witch exists, should ya really go tamperin' with somethin' like that, kid? It looks kinda... stuck in there," Buffoh said, leaning away as he pointed at the boy's chest.

"It doesn't matter anymore," Arden replied with defeat. "I've already found her."

"You did?" Vee asked.

"She's real?!" Buffoh shouted.

Gord's face lit up with surprise as he signed, *What happened? What did she say?*

Arden huffed. "She couldn't remove the stone."

"Did she at least tell ya anything about it?" Buffoh asked, itching for more information on the witch.

"She recited some sort of prophecy, but it was very confusing," the boy said. "She spoke about embodiments of life and death, souls that remained, and some beast to defeat—a creature that could kill Elves. I don't know—at times, I could barely tell if she was talking about the past or the future."

"Well, why don't we go back to her? Maybe she can give a better explanation," Vee suggested.

Arden shook his head vigorously.

"No way!" he replied. "She wanted to take my stone and eat me alive. I barely escaped with my life. Besides, I've already got enough people chasing after me."

"Ah, so that's where the bird lady comes in," Buffoh surmised.

"Is that Or'Ackin woman after your stone, Arden?" Vee asked.

"Yes," the boy replied, "and before you ask—no, I don't know why. But she's been following me for days now."

"This ain't good, kid," Buffoh said with worry. "Gettin' hunted by someone like her... I'm amazed ya haven't been caught yet."

"Me too," Arden admitted.

There was silence again. A grim feeling filled the air until Vee asked, "So... what now?"

Arden and Gord looked at one another, unsure as well.

"I don't know," the boy said. "I mean, we can't even go back home. That Or'Ackin knows where we live."

Gord placed a hand on his son's shoulder, his eyes tender with sorrow.

Vee thought for a moment, then said, "Come with me to Haroon."

"What?" Arden asked.

"Come with me. You said you have nowhere else to go, right? Well, Buffoh and I are heading there anyway. You might as well join us. And if we get to Haroon and you don't like it, you can always go somewhere else. But who knows? Maybe it'll be a fresh start for you guys."

Arden and his father considered the idea.

"Would that be alright with you?" the boy asked, turning to Buffoh.

"No skin off my rump. I mean, normally, I'd charge ya extra for all this, but to be honest, I just wanna get out of this place. I'm chaffin' over here," the Leptoid said, fixing his pants.

Gord patted his son's back and gave a nod.

"It's settled, then. To Haroon," said Vee.

For the remainder of the night, they trekked through the swamp with Buffoh as their guide. The Leptoid was overly-cautious the whole time, pointing out every spiddle root and crog nest along the way.

Exhaustion weighed heavily on the travelers, but there was barely enough time to eat, let alone sleep. And though Arden was tired, he was more concerned with the Or'Ackin on their trail than anything else. The boy peeked around every corner, paranoid she'd be lurking nearby.

After a while, his eyes began to play tricks on him, conjuring up visions of faces in the darkness ahead. Whether it was sleep deprivation or just the swamp's games, he couldn't tell, but Arden knew he needed to get out of there soon.

As the boy was about to give up all faith, there was a glint in the distance. Arden nearly dismissed it as another hallucination, but the shimmer persisted. Could it be?

He sprinted ahead of his companions, eager to know if the sun had finally risen, dying to feel its warmth on his clammy face.

Every step brought more into view until the rays of daylight were beaming all around him, illuminating every leaf and rock.

"We've made it! It's morning!" he shouted back to his friends as they rushed behind him.

Up ahead, Arden could see the edge of the swamp, its treeline ending like a sudden wall.

His entire body pumped with excitement, but as he reached the last few trees of the forest, his legs went as stiff as boards. The boy skidded to a grinding halt, but the pebbles at his feet kept rolling forward, falling off a cliff and down into the raging waters below.

Arden glanced around, shocked to have almost plummeted to his doom but eager to find some way across the canyon. A terrible emptiness ached within as he began to recognize his surroundings.

Arched over the rapids sat an old and rotting tree bridge, its roots digging into the walls of the cliff like fingers.

"No," he whispered in disbelief. "How did we end up *here*?!"

As his fellow travelers arrived, they too were met with equal feelings of despair by the familiar sight.

They were right back where they'd started: the entrance of Blackwater Swamp.

A steady growl rumbled from behind Vee's lips.

"I can't believe you messed this up again, Buffoh!" she snapped.

The Leptoid scoffed.

"Well, it ain't like I had a map to follow!" he shouted back. "You should consider yaselves lucky I got us out of there at all."

"Lucky?" Arden asked. "You were supposed to bring us to Haroon! How do you expect us to—"

"There you are!" boomed a proud voice from across the canyon.

Arden and his friends fell silent, drawing their attention to the opposite side of the bridge. There, a towering man sat atop a massive, red-haired bull-pig. Two deer horns protruded from the warrior's bark helmet, and an ancient ax was holstered over his red cape. Behind him, a battalion of twenty knights riding smaller bull-pigs emerged from the trees, forming two perfect ranks.

"Finally!" the man said. "I was beginning to worry you'd never make it out of there. We've spent days searching for you, and here you stand."

Arden remained still.

"Kid, you know this guy?" Buffoh asked.

Arden slowly shook his head. His focus honed in on the antlered man in the distance.

"Oh, forgive me," the general said, noticing the boy's perplexed face. "I'm not used to introducing myself. I am Zark, lord and savior of Dacarr. And you must be the Elf who's carrying the stone."

The boy tensed.

"I don't know what you're talking about," he yelled across the river. "You must be mistaking me for someone else!"

Zark sighed.

"No, I don't think I am. You're Arden. From Noakwood Hollow," he said with confidence. "We've come a long way to find you, boy. Even paid a visit to a friend of yours at Mogoroth—Finn, was it?" He glanced over to Commander Tull for confirmation.

"Yes, Lord Zark," she replied with a stern nod.

Arden remained quiet, shaking his head in disbelief.

"I'll admit, that gutless Noamin put up quite a fight... at first. But you'll find I have a way of making people come around. By the end of our little chat, that fool practically screamed everything we needed to hear," Zark said, enjoying the boy's growing rage.

"What did you do to him?" Arden asked, curling his fists.

Zark chuckled, as did some of his soldiers.

"Hardly the question," the warlord said, his grin falling humorless. "Finn sold you out—mentioned your journey to the swamp—a brave undertaking, I must say. Although, I suppose we shouldn't give all the credit to that coward. It seems we had some help from another 'friend' of yours... if *that's* what you call these people."

Zark waved his hand at Arden's companions. "You have nowhere to run to now. Step forward. Show him who you *really* are!"

The boy turned to Buffoh first with an expression beyond puzzlement. "What is he talking about?"

"Ay, don't look at me!" the Leptoid protested. "I've never met this guy."

Arden drew his attention to Vee at the back of the group next. Her posture was shrunken, her eyes glassy and full of guilt.

"That's right," Zark said with a devious smirk. "If it wasn't for our little Dacarri rebel here, we may never have found you. You're quite good at hiding your tracks, boy... but she's not. Isn't that right, Delvina?"

Gord's brow flew high, and he took a step back.

"I knew she had a weird name," Buffoh said, crossing his arms. "I said it, didn't I? Didn't I say it? I knew it."

"Delvina?" Arden repeated. "Y-you're with him?"

"No, Arden. I'm—"

"With me?" Zark interjected. "That girl is a pathetic traitor. She will never be considered a Dacarri again, not under my rule. She belongs to no people, not even her own, now."

Vee shied away.

Arden placed a hand on his temple, trying to grasp the situation. "You're a Dacarri? But you said you were an Elf."

"I'm not an Elf, and I'm not from Rook," Vee admitted somberly. "I come from a long line of Dacarri rebels. We've been fighting Zark and his army for years. But everything else I've told you is true. I would never work for Zark. He's the one who slashed my leg—the one who murdered my parents. He's the man I've been running from this whole time. I couldn't reveal who I really was, or he might've found me. But I swear I thought he was only following *me*. I had no idea he was searching for *you*."

Arden studied Vee's eyes intently, seeing the truth within them. Despite feeling disappointment over her secrecy, that emotion quickly gave way to guilt. He too had kept secrets to protect himself. At that moment, he realized just how much they shared. They were both victims in their own right, fleeing from hunters who had upended their lives.

Zark angrily shouted from across the canyon once more, "My patience is wearing thin, boy, and I am not known for mercy. But if you turn yourself over to me now, I'll spare your friends—even that rebel."

Vee whispered over the boy's shoulder, "Don't listen to him. He'll take your stone, then kill the rest of us anyway."

Arden bit his lip, his mind racing for a solution.

"And if I were to surrender," he yelled back to the tyrant, "how can I trust you'll keep your word?"

"You can't," Zark replied.

"So, what's to stop us from running back into the swamp, then?"

A thunderous roar suddenly erupted through the canyon, sending a shiver down the boy's spine.

Turning their attention to the familiar gloom of the swamp, Arden and the others saw the Or'Ackin sorceress mounted atop her vile gringore, lurking in the shadows.

"Welp, so much for that," Buffoh said.

Zark leered at the masked woman.

"Ah, Rue'Na," he said, craning his neck. "I had a feeling your people would send out a sorcerer to claim what's rightfully mine. Although, I wasn't exactly certain... given that there aren't many of your kind left to take up the task."

The sorceress glared at the warlord with her ghostly white eyes, then said, "What lies with the boy belongs to the Or'Ackins."

"No," Zark replied. "Your people had their chance, and they failed. The Or'Ackins are weaker than they've ever been. I will not see the stone tainted by the likes of you again, witch!"

A vicious snarl escaped Rue'Na's lips. She steered her ravenous gringore into the daylight, heading right for Arden.

The boy took note of the tight swamp vines wrapped around the sorceress's legs, securing her to the creature. There would be no chance of her falling off the beast this time.

Arden and his allies backed away with every step the gringore took, forced to the center of the decaying bridge.

Zark commanded his bull-pig forward at the sight of Rue'Na's advance. As he too stepped onto the bridge, the bark beneath everyone's feet began to crack.

"I've heard such claims before when I agreed to help your people eleven years ago," he shouted to the sorceress, ignoring the debris now crumbling off the bridge. "But now, a debt is owed to me. You will surrender the stone as payment."

Rue'Na unsheathed the boomerang from her belt, gripping it tightly. The sharp stone blade glowed red with an intense heat.

"Then you will have to pry it from my dead hands," she hissed.

Zark gave a sarcastic chuckle. He seized the double-bladed ax from behind his back, raising it to the cloudy sky.

"Borka, father of all Dacarri," he chanted, gazing into the weapon's orange gem. "Grant me the fire of your might. Alight this ax with your fury!"

Like magic, scorching flames ignited the weapon's stone blades, burning brighter than the sorceress's boomerang.

Rue'Na whipped her gringore, charging for Arden and his friends.

Zark's bull-pig barreled forward as the Dacarri knights watched from the cliff.

Arden shut his eyes, pressing his back against his father.

Just as the two hunters reached the center of the bridge, Gord wrapped his massive arms around his son and the others. With a great leap, he jumped for the rapids below.

A deafening rumble echoed above them as the bridge collapsed into a hundred giant splinters.

Rue'Na and Zark plummeted amidst the debris as Gord and his fellow travelers crashed into the water first.

The harsh waves tossed Arden about as he emerged from the surface, gasping for breath. Spotting a large chunk of the bridge floating downstream, he called out to his friends, "Quick, climb onto that log!"

The group swam for the raft, their feet slipping on its slick bark as they tried to pull themselves up to safety. Gaining his footing, Buffoh mounted the front of the log as Gord and Mugz climbed on behind him. Arden followed shortly after, turning around to help Vee.

As the girl took a seat on the raft, she reached down into the water and pulled out a branch.

"Grab a hold of something to paddle with!" she shouted.

Using various pieces of the shattered bridge, the travelers navigated frantically as the current pulled them down the river. They weaved around rocks and jagged turns, their movements desperate and erratic.

"We're never gonna make it outta this thing!" Buffoh screamed.

"Don't say that," Arden replied. "We just need to keep—"

A ferocious yell bellowed from behind. Zark was barreling toward them, his bull-pig swimming with great speed.

Gripping his mount's saddle with one hand, the tyrant drew his flaming ax in the other.

Chanting resounded from the cliffs above as his knights followed along its very edge through the woods, glancing down at the scene in the river.

As the shadow of a double-headed ax drifted across his father's back, Arden screamed, "Get down!"

The boy and his friends ducked, narrowly avoiding Zark's wide swing.

The bitter scent of smoke filled the air, and the blood-thirsty warlord raised his ax once more, this time aiming only for Arden.

"The stone is mine!" he shouted.

Defenseless, the boy froze, clutching his paddle. He braced for the slash of Zark's fiery ax but instead heard a chilling roar echo beside him.

Suddenly, a colossal thud shifted the raft to the left as Rue'Na's gringore latched onto the rear.

Zark swung down, narrowly missing Arden by a hair. Still fixated on the boy, he failed to notice the imposing rocks ahead. With a loud crash, his bull-pig slammed against them, harshly launching the armored tyrant off his saddle and into the boulders.

Commander Tull came to a halt on the cliffs above. Retrieving some rope, she looked down at her struggling leader, seemingly hesitant to lower it down.

"What are you waiting for, Commander?" one of the soldiers beside her shouted.

Tull watched as Arden and his fellowship were carried further downstream, then finally tossed the rope to her injured leader.

Rue'Na's gringore regained its balance and began to crawl up the travelers' raft, drawing Arden's attention once more. The log capsized under the weight of the heavy beast, forcing its passengers to slide down. While Arden, Gord, and Buffoh held on tight, Vee struggled to find a good grip.

Arden turned back, extending his hand to aid the girl, but before she could reach him, the loud crack of Rue'Na's whip pierced the air.

In an instant, Vee's leg was ensnared by the wicked sorceress, and she yanked the girl toward her.

"No!" Arden cried.

Vee slid down the log but dug her nails into the bark to stop herself. She clawed forward, trying to reach Arden once more, but Rue'Na's whip was still wrapped around her leg.

"Attempting to flee an Or'Ackin?" the sorceress snickered, lifting her red-hot boomerang for the strike. "No one shall escape me again—not even you!"

Vee grabbed a dagger from her belt and hurled it straight for Rue'Na.

As the blade sliced through the woman's arm, a plume of black ash poured from the wound, wisping off into the air. Rue'Na let out a horrible shriek, peering upon the gash. She pulled her whip from Vee's leg and snapped it beside the gringore, commanding it forward.

Already holding her last dagger, Vee threw it at the beast's face.

The blade slashed across the gringore's eye, and it leaped from the raft with a roar, plunging into the water. The sudden movement rocked the log, sending a wave of water over the travelers.

Rue'Na tried to gain control of her steed, but the writhing creature refused to obey. Instead, it swam for the walls of the canyon and crawled back up to the cliffside in agony.

Vee managed to climb her way back up their raft.

"You alright?" Arden asked.

"Yes," the girl panted, brushing the wet hair from her face. "That was close."

Finally free from the hunters, Arden, and his friends watched as the sorceress and her gringore disappeared into the swamp above. But Buffoh was focused on something else.

"Ya's may not wanna hear this," he screamed, "but we're headin' straight for rocks!"

The travelers spun back around to see a barricade of enormous boulders jutting out in every direction. There was no way through.

"We have to turn around!" Arden shouted, frantically sweeping his paddle through the water.

Gord pushed hard against the current with a large branch, managing to spin the raft all the way around, but it wasn't enough to slow their speed.

The rapids grew stronger, pulling their log toward the jagged stone teeth of the river.

Just as they were about to collide, a loud explosion boomed from atop the canyon, and a tree came crashing down between their raft and the rocks.

Chapter 19

THE CITY BENEATH THE HILL

The stern of the travelers' raft smashed into the fallen tree, jolting everyone backward.

From the top of the southern cliffside, a man's voice echoed, "Don't just sit there. Get up, all of you! Climb across the tree!"

Arden's gaze drifted upward, catching a glimpse of the mysterious man above them. The boy flinched as he recognized the bronze hook hanging from the stranger's right sleeve. It was the hooded scavenger who'd dropped the spark bark days ago.

"Who is *this* now?" Buffoh asked, voicing the question on everyone's mind.

"I don't know," the boy admitted.

"Arden, you must come with me," the stranger urgently called out. "I've been protecting you since you left Mogoroth to journey north—I saved you from Rue'Na that night in the woods."

Arden's thoughts raced with memories of the sorceress's boomerang nearly cutting him down on that misty night. Yes, this man saved him, but who was he really? For all Arden knew, he could be another seeker of the stone, and judging by the wary expressions on his companions' faces, they were thinking the same thing.

Suddenly, the thunderous pounding of bull-pigs echoed from the west. Arden turned to see Zark and his knights charging along the cliffside. A swirling could of dust trailed behind them as their voices rose in a menacing chant.

"Either come with me or die here!" the hook-handed man shouted, crouching out of sight from the Dacarri approaching.

Arden hesitated, but there were only two options: take the hook-handed man up on his offer or suffer the blade of a fiery ax.

"He's right," Arden said, quickly assessing the situation. "We need to hurry. Go!"

Scrambling onto the fallen tree, the travelers climbed across to join the hooded stranger. As they reached the top of the cliffside, the man lent his hand to help them.

Vee, being the first to reach him, glared with distrust but grabbed his forearm and pulled herself up.

One by one, Arden and his team gathered on the edge of the cliff.

"Quickly, now. There is no more time," the scavenger said, running ahead into Feverwood Forest.

Arden scanned his group as the sound of Zark and his knights drew near.

"Let's go," said the boy with uncertainty, following behind the stranger.

As the travelers ran west through the woods, time seemed to blur. Their lungs burned, and their legs ached, yet still, the scavenger urged them forward, never slowing.

Only when the trees thinned into a small clearing did he finally come to a halt. The man turned to face them, ensuring no one had fallen behind.

"Good, you're all here," he said.

Gasping for breath, Arden held his knees.

"My apologies for approaching you like this," the man continued. "It's not what I had hoped for—believe me."

The stranger removed his scarf and hood, unveiling two pointed ears beneath his wavy black hair. A long beard hung down from his slender face.

Arden lifted his head, surprised to see the stranger was a middle-aged Elf.

"I suppose now I should introduce myself," the man said. "My name is Zolan. I was a mage from the fallen city of Elbrith... and an old friend of your family, Arden."

Gord and his son glared at one another, suspicious of the man's claims.

Arden replied, "I was raised by Gord. *He's* my family."

Zolan lowered his head, keeping his eyes fixed on the boy. "Well, surely you must have come from Elves at *some* point, no?"

Arden felt a touch of confusion and curiosity at Zolan's question. Being raised by Gord, an Ogre who had always been kind and protective, Arden never gave much thought to where he had come from or who his real parents might've been. The boy recalled the few times he had attempted to ask his father about the past. Gord would always grow somber and sign, It *doesn't matter where you come from. What matters is who you choose to be.*

But now, standing before Zolan, Arden felt a new urgency to know. There was a part of him that yearned for answers, to understand the truth about his heritage. Did this man truly know his parents?

Zolan continued, "I know you're eager to hear more, but there will be plenty of time to explain everything later. For now, we must continue west. We cannot allow Rue'Na or Zark to acquire your stone—"

"Whoa, hang on there," Buffoh said quickly. "Kid, are ya sure we should be followin' this guy in the first place? This all seems kinda sudden."

"Yes, and how do we know if we can even trust him?" Vee added. "It may look like he saved us, but what if he's just luring us into some trap?"

The mage tensed.

Arden looked up at his doubtful father, then back to Zolan.

"They're right," Arden said. "Why should I take your word? I can't just follow some stranger who knows my name. I mean, I've become quite popular across Cynorrum lately. For all I know, you could have learned about me through anyone. And you say you know my birth family, but why should I believe that? What if you're just after my stone?"

"That couldn't be further from the truth," Zolan said firmly. "If I wanted the stone, I would have taken it by now. Plenty of opportunities have presented themselves. There's no doubt about that. I don't wish to take it—I seek to protect it, and you."

Arden shook his head, eyeing the ground.

Zolan huffed. "Arden... I was there when that stone was

placed into your chest eleven years ago."

The boy stood straight. How could this man possibly know that? Finn was right all along—someone *had* given him the stone deliberately.

"Listen, I want to trust you. I do," Arden said. "But I need a good enough reason."

Zolan thought for a moment, then asked, "Tell me, when the Ogre found you... was it by a river near Aramore?"

Arden and his father turned to one another as a wave of shock came over them both. No one could have known such a thing unless they were there themselves that night.

The mage turned to Gord. "He was wounded when you'd found him, wasn't he? Wrapped in bloodied rags?"

The Ogre stared at him in disbelief, then gave the slightest nod.

"I know you're probably confused, Arden," Zolan continued, turning back to the boy. "I didn't want to do this here and now, but we can discuss it further once we've reached Dwyn."

Vee stepped forward.

"Dwyn? What's that?" she asked.

"It's from a children's story," Buffoh chimed in with a judging tone. "Some ancient city buried under the ground, yada, yada. It's just a myth."

Zolan regarded the Leptoid sharply. "What are myths if not forgotten history? Dwyn is as real as the grass beneath our feet. And I would know, for I had discovered its abandoned caverns ages ago when I was a much younger Elf."

"Oh, whatever!" Buffoh said, waving a hand. "That's great and all, but I still ain't followin' somebody I just met." The Leptoid walked over to Arden, his chin up high. "Look,

I got ya through the swamp, just like ya asked. And now, I'm done. That's it for me."

"What?" Arden asked, surprised as Buffoh began to walk away. "After all of this, you're just going to leave?"

"Hello! And what about me?" Vee asked. "I still have to get to Haroon!"

"Ay!" Buffoh snapped, halting in his tracks to face the confused bunch. "Our deal ended when we left that swamp. As far as I'm concerned, lady, ya on your own. And kid, good luck with that weird stone thing ya got. I'm goin' back to Anura. Take care!"

As the Leptoid turned once more, Zolan said, "You can't leave, toad. In fact, none of you can. We are all marked. If any of you were to go off on your own, Rue'Na or Zark would surely find and torture you for information or use you as leverage to get to Arden. We can't afford that."

Buffoh paused again, his back still turned, grumbling with his arms crossed. "Damn it!" he muttered, realizing the mage had a point.

Arden bit his lip, still skeptical about the whole thing. He looked to Gord for some wisdom on what to do, but it seemed the Ogre was just as unsure. They silently weighed their options, realizing there was only one choice: they had to follow Zolan.

"Alright," Arden said, glancing back at the mage with grave acceptance. "Take us to Dwyn."

Zolan nodded solemnly. "Before we start our journey, there is something we must do first."

"And what might that be?" Vee asked.

"Zark and Rue'Na are likely following our trail this very minute," Zolan replied. "We must mask our scent to hinder them from finding us. I have something that can help, but it's in short supply, I'm afraid."

The mage revealed a belt beneath his dusted cloak, adorned with strange bottles and potions from various regions. He rifled through them until his fingers met a small glass jar filled with a dry, ancient-looking dust.

"What I hold before you is powdered anula root," he said, presenting the jar. "Its aroma matches that of dirt—stronger, even. It should keep us hidden from the gringore and Zark's bull-pigs for a while. Now, hold out your hands and apply this to the bottom of your shoes."

The boy and his friends reached out, and Zolan distributed a small portion of the powder to each of them.

"Oh, it smells awful," Buffoh muttered as he and the others coated their heels. "Stupid hunters, makin' us have to rub this crap on ourselves. Ya know what? I don't smell now, right?! They can't track me. So, I can head back home, yes?"

Zolan gave the Leptoid a hard stare. "Not a chance. Even with this powder, you won't have long until those hunters catch up to you. Anura village is much farther than this scent will last."

Buffoh glared at the mage, grumbling under his breath.

"If we head to Dwyn now, we could reach its gates in just over a day," Zolan said. "We should be safe in its hollows. Now, come along."

Vee and Buffoh followed as the mage began to lead them through the forest, but Gord turned to Arden and signed, *Is this what you want? We can still go our own way.*

Arden motioned back. *I'm not so sure we have a choice. If he claims to know a safe place, then it's our best chance.*

The Ogre sighed, placing a hand on the boy's shoulder as they too fell in line behind Zolan and the others.

Their journey through Feverwood Forest stretched long and quiet. Though Zolan led the way with confidence, he spoke very little, offering only an occasional direction or hushed warning. The group, weary from travel and their looming pursuit, rarely broke the silence themselves.

During the brief hours Zolan allowed them to rest, Arden caught a glimpse of him—wide-eyed and scanning the darkened woods. The mage held his potions close, ready for anything that dwelled within their midst.

An entire day passed as the travelers ventured alongside the mysterious man. On that following evening, they had come to a large hill in the southern half of Feverwood Forest. Before them sat a gigantic wall of jagged boulders, overgrown with years of vines and foliage.

"Yes. This is it," Zolan whispered aloud, his voice carrying a hint of anticipation. He placed a tender hand on the stone wall. "The secret entrance to Dwyn. It's just behind these rocks."

Arden and his fellow journeyers stared at the wall from afar.

"So?" the boy asked. "How do we get in?"

Zolan rubbed his chin in thought. "Well, if I'm remembering correctly, we need to touch these four stones in a particular order, and the door should open. Once it does, we'll have only a few moments to step inside and travel the tunnel before it seals shut again."

"Seals shut?" Vee asked, anxiously gazing at the rock wall.

"Yes, so we must be swift," Zolan replied. "Now, brace yourselves. This may be loud."

The travelers plugged their ears as Zolan began to press against a few rocks with his palm. Then, the mage quickly hopped away from the wall in the hillside.

Arden and the others froze in wonder, waiting for a terrible noise to follow, but nothing happened.

"Ya sure ya been here before?" Buffoh asked, breaking the tension.

"Don't be ridiculous! Of course, I have," Zolan said. "I used ancient scrolls to find this gate last time, so I'm certain this is the entrance."

The mage examined the boulders more carefully. "I must have touched the stones in the wrong pattern, that's all. Now, let me think. How did that riddle go again?"

He pondered for a moment until his eyes went aglow with recollection. He placed a palm on a stone to the right, then moved to one on the left, reciting,

"Moons of east,
Fade to west..."

He touched another stone up high.

Zolan knelt and placed his hand on a smoother rock near the bottom of the wall.

In seconds, the ground shook with a heavy rumble, and the vines covering the rocks slithered into the cracks of the hill. The four enormous stones slid apart in their respective directions, revealing a dark cave behind them.

"See? Just as I told you," Zolan said, hurrying into the black. "Now, come on!"

Arden and his friends hesitated, uncertain of what might be waiting for them inside. A damp, musty air drifted out from the cave, carrying the scent of a place undisturbed for ages. A sickening chill ran down the travelers' spines.

The stony entrance groaned once more as the jagged boulders began their slow, grinding return. Dust billowed out as the gap between the stones shrank.

Zolan nervously glanced over his shoulder at the rocks and cried, "What are you standing around for? You don't have much time. Hurry!"

In a panic, the group snapped from their hesitation and bolted forward, racing to the closing passage. The two main boulders were about to come together again, and the travelers slipped inside just as the door sealed itself shut. A thunderous boom quaked behind them.

Immediately, the vines of the hillside slithered back into their original positions, as if the wall had been untouched for centuries.

An awkward silence filled the air as everyone remained

still in the pitch black.

"Well... it's dark," said Vee, her voice bouncing throughout the cavern.

Nothing was visible, but they could hear the eerie plink of water droplets echoing further off.

Everyone shuffled about to gain their bearings, but it was simply too dark to make sense of anything.

"Zolan?" Arden whispered, trying to find the mage in the void.

"I'm here."

"Where do we go?" the boy asked, blindly feeling his way forward.

"We should've lit a torch," Buffoh remarked.

"Oh, look. Someone finally learned something," Vee quipped.

"What's that supposed to mean?"

"Forget it."

"Quiet," Zolan said. "We'll be out of here soon. If my memory serves correctly, we should end up at the main cavern hall. It's well-lit. Just continue forward."

"Forward?" Buffoh asked, feeling around with his feet. "I wouldn't have to worry *where* forward was if we just lit a damn torch—"

As the Leptoid stepped onto an oddly-smooth rock, it sank into the floor. A series of muffled taps resounded beneath his feet, followed by a loud crack.

Suddenly, the floor opened up, swallowing the travelers whole. Their screams echoed as they plummeted deep into the ground.

Chapter 20

THE FATE OF TWO HEARTS

Arden and his companions tumbled through the winding tunnel until they finally landed on the cold, rocky ground of a dimly lit cavern. Groans of discomfort filled the room as they gathered themselves.

"How did you forget a drop like *that*?" Arden asked Zolan as he rubbed his aching head.

"Sorry," the mage replied. "It's been a while."

As they recovered from the fall, the group took in the unfamiliar surroundings. The walls of the chamber were riddled with passageways, each leading into an ominously dark shaft.

"Look there!" Zolan exclaimed, pointing toward one of the tunnels. "We've made it."

At the end of the passage was a bright glow shining from a hidden room to the right. The mage rushed into it as Arden and his friends followed with caution.

"Just through here," Zolan said, disappearing into the light of the chamber.

Arden and the others wondered if they all shared the same feelings of apprehension. Could this have been a trap? It was rather odd that a cave would be so well-lit, especially given it was abandoned. Perhaps it *wasn't*, after all.

"No point in turning back now, right?" Vee asked nervously.

Despite their discomfort, the journeyers pressed onward and walked through the entryway. As their eyes ad-
justed to the radiant cavern, relief washed over them.

This was no elaborate ruse but a wondrous scene. The
travelers had stepped onto a stone balcony overlooking a
colossal cave. Light poured from giant glowing crystals embedded in the ceiling, illuminating the vast garden
sprawled across the cavern floor. Clear streams glistened
as they wove beneath the trunks of golden trees while vi-
brant flowers dotted the hills far and wide.

Arden approached the railing of the stone ledge, capti-
vated by the brilliance.

"Amazing, isn't it?" Zolan remarked.

"It's incredible," Vee whispered, her eyes fixed on the
crystal ceiling.

"Well, I guess it is real
then," Buffoh grum-
bled, sounding more
annoyed about be-
ing wrong than
anything else.

"Quite," Zolan re-
sponded. "Though it's
merely a shadow of what
it used to be. These cav-
erns were once home to
the Muskers—a society
of rodent people: skilled
miners and herbalists."

"Muskers? I think
I've seen one of them

212

before at Mogoroth," Arden said.

"I'm surprised. Muskers tend to stay away from lively markets. Since leaving Dwyn, they've rarely been seen."

"Why'd they leave?" Vee asked.

"Not sure. There's little record of their departure," Zolan replied. "This city hasn't been inhabited for centuries, so we'll have a safe place to rest."

The mage inspected the cave once more, noticing another hallway at the left end of the balcony.

"I believe the old sleeping quarters are over there," he said. "Perhaps it's time we got off our feet, no?"

Arden and his friends agreed.

Following Zolan, they moved away from the balcony and strolled to the corridor. The passage was wide and dark, but the air grew cooler as they walked.

Eventually, they emerged into another circular chamber. In this room, hundreds of tiny yellow crystals were scattered throughout the rocky walls, filling the space with a warm glow. The floor's perimeter had been lined with beds made from giant mushroom caps. There were ten in all, each uniquely sized but perfectly suited for everyone, even Mugz.

"Don't mind if I do!" said Buffoh, leaping right onto one of the caps.

The rest of the group proceeded to lounge on the soft fungi as well, attempting to get a good night's sleep.

Gord, however, seemed the least eager to rest. Arden could see from the corner of his eye the giant observing Zolan with a judgmental gaze as he lay upon one of the mushroom beds.

Curious, the boy softly snapped his fingers to get his father's attention.

What is it? Arden signed.

Gord's expression hardened for a moment. *I'm doubtful of what this mage claims to know. What if he isn't who he says he is? Or worse, what if he tries to take you away from me?*

Arden's heart ached as he watched Gord's eyes well up.

Why would he do that? the boy signed back.

If he truly knows your real family, he might try and—Gord began, but Arden interjected.

Don't worry. No matter what Zolan tells me, you'll always be my father.

The Ogre took a deep breath, appearing calmer from his son's reassurance.

With a somber smile, Arden rested his head.

The next morning, the boy arose slowly, bellowing a deep yawn as he gazed around the room. His friends were still sound asleep. Mugz was curled up into a tight ball while Buffoh sprawled across his bed. Vee and Gord lay on their sides, their backs turned.

Arden let out another soft breath. Then, he noticed Zolan sitting beside him on one of the mushroom caps, silently writing in a journal.

The boy rubbed his eyes, feeling a bit disoriented. "How long have I been asleep?" he asked.

Zolan glanced up, closing the book and sliding it into his cloak.

"A while," he replied. "It's far past noon, I'd imagine. But you clearly needed the rest."

Arden nodded. "I'm just glad we're safe. I feel like I can finally breathe again, especially knowing Zark and Rue'Na won't be able to find us here."

Zolan's expression darkened. "Well... for a time, anyway."

"What?" Arden asked, puzzled. "I thought you said the anula root would mask our scent."

The mage gave a heavy sigh, his head hanging to the floor. "It should have, but I can't be so sure. If the effects wore off too soon, we could still be found. Let's hope that wasn't the case, for our sake and the stone's."

"Yes, let's hope," Arden agreed anxiously.

Zolan stared at him for a moment, a grim look in his eye. He didn't say a word, but Arden could sense the man's fears growing.

"I don't understand something," the boy continued. "What makes this stone so valuable that people are seeking me out for it? Wh-what is this thing?"

The mage tapped his hook in thought, then rose to his feet.

"Come with me. I'll explain," he said.

Arden eagerly hopped off the bed, torn between feelings of excitement and terror. This was it, the moment he'd dreamed about and dreaded all at once. What if the truth was something he couldn't handle? What if it was more than he had ever imagined—or less? His mind swirled with questions and fears.

Arden glanced at his friends on the mushroom beds, their peaceful faces an utter contrast to the unease swirling within him. Careful not to wake them, the boy tiptoed out of the room. He felt a touch of guilt for leaving without a word, but this was something he needed to face alone.

As Zolan led the way, Arden followed close behind, his thoughts spiraling deeper with every step.

After a brief stroll through the tunnels, they arrived

back at the massive gardens of the grand cavern. Descending a wide staircase carved into the rock walls, they stepped down into the large expanse of greenery stretching ahead. The trickle of flowing streams sang gently through the air, easing Arden's anxious mind.

Zolan walked over to a stone bench at the center of the chamber, its surface smooth from centuries of use. He took a seat, gesturing for the boy to join him.

Arden hesitated but sat beside the mage.

There was a brief moment of silence between the two Elves before Zolan said, "I know why you've traveled all this way. Venturing to find The Witch of Blackwater Swamp was brave but foolish. I'm still amazed you escaped."

The boy slouched, uncertain if he should feel embarrassed or proud.

"I was desperate," he admitted. "I just needed answers."

"And did you find what you were looking for?" the mage asked. "Did you find the witch?"

"I did," Arden said, nervously picking the edge of the stone bench. "And she told me a prophecy, but... in riddles."

"What did she mention?"

"Something about embodiments of life and death and souls that remained in stone. I didn't know what to make of it."

"I'm sure you didn't," Zolan replied with a nod. "But whatever the witch told you is undoubtedly true."

The boy raised a brow. "You know what she meant by all that?"

"I do," Zolan admitted, pulling the old notebook from his cloak. He flipped through it, looking for the correct page. "And what she told you is a history of sorts—a story that spans thousands of years and one that I believe is intertwined with your own."

Arden frowned, trying to make sense of the mage's assumption. "What do you mean?"

Zolan hesitated, sifting through the pages until he'd found a sketch resembling the natural elements. A series of lines branched out from each symbol, connecting to drawings of various peoples.

"Arden, every group of beings you can think of, from Elves to Ogres, began with a single person among them known as a Prime. These individuals were capable of extraordinary magic."

He flipped to the next page, which depicted two opposing figures: one radiating light and the other shrouded in darkness. "The Elves and the Or'Ackins boasted the two most powerful of these beings. Our Prime could restore health to whatever they wished, and in contrast, the Or'Ackins' could take it away."

"Embodiments of life and death," Arden thought aloud, a slight chill running down his spine as he looked upon the drawings.

"Exactly," the mage continued, tapping the page. "When the Prime Elf and Or'Ackin perished, their magical hearts remained and transformed into rock."

He flipped again, revealing an illustration of two stones, one elegant with a clean outline and the other shaded in gray smudges. "They were later named the Everstone and the Grimstone."

Arden moved a hand to his chest, feeling the scar beneath his shirt.

"The Everstone?" he asked, glancing at the elegant rock sketched in the journal. "Is that what I carry?"

Zolan nodded.

"Wait," the boy said, looking at his torso. "So, that means I have a dead person's heart lodged in my chest?"

"Precisely."

Arden tried to stay calm over such an unsettling fact.

"Alright," he said. "If I have the Everstone, then where's the Grimstone?"

Zolan closed his notebook and looked off, a pitiful expression washing over his face. "The Or'Ackins claimed it shortly after their Prime's death, just as the Elves did with the Everstone. Though, for the Or'Ackins, that was a grave mistake. The Grimstone would plague their home, Havarria, for generations to come."

Arden's eyes went aglow with a sudden memory. "Wait! Gord told me about their lands once. He said it was a place of eternal night and snow. That's because of the Grimstone, isn't it?"

"Yes. It drained Havarria of life."

"And what about the Or'Ackins?"

A sigh left Zolan's bearded lips. He arose from the bench and walked ahead to a small fountain sitting beneath a yellow-leafed tree. The mage placed his hands on the cracked rim, tracing his fingers across the once-beautiful structure.

"It cursed them—devoured their souls," he said, staring into the dried basin. "Not only did it turn their skin blue, eyes white, and blood to ash... but worst of all, it has diminished their ability to breed. They are a dying people, Arden."

The boy sat in silence, stunned. A stone that could curse an entire group of people? It almost seemed impossible.

Zolan continued, "The Or'Ackins are desperate, and *that* is perhaps the most terrifying thing about them. Desperation can cause people to do wicked and terrible things."

A single leaf, brown and shriveled, fell from a branch dangling above the mage's head. It settled among a small pile of rotted leaves converging at the center of the fountain. Zolan's eyes followed its quiet descent as if the leaf were the Or'Ackins' own decline.

"Hey," Arden said, drawing the mage's attention. "If the Grimstone's power was able to curse the Or'Ackins, then what about my stone?"

Zolan drew his hands off the fountain and turned with a narrowed stare.

"Tell me... just how far back can you remember?" he asked.

The question caught Arden by surprise.

"Oh, well... I only remember my life with Gord. He said I must've been about four years old when he found me. Apparently, I couldn't recall anything except my name."

Zolan remained stoic and said, "Ages ago, our people acquired the Everstone, hid it beneath the mountains, and built a kingdom atop it, Elbrith—the city where you were born."

"The city where *I* was born?" Arden asked.

"Yes—before it came to ruin," Zolan replied sadly. "Elbrith once flourished from the Everstone's power, which gave the Elves incredible health and vitality... even yourself."

Arden sat straight as he finally understood why his wounds disappeared overnight. Gord always told him he was an unusually fast healer, but now it all made sense. The boy began to wonder how else the stone might've been affecting him.

He thought back to a night long ago when he fell from a tree and broke his arm, only to wake up the next morning with nothing but a minor ache. He remembered the countless injuries that vanished within hours, like the cut he had acquired at Aramore or the blisters he'd gotten from the cave slime. Each incident had seemed miraculous, but now he saw the common thread: the Everstone.

"So, this stone," Arden said, pinching the space between his eyes. "It's been healing me? Keeping me alive?"

Zolan nodded. "The Everstone's magic flows through you, sustaining your life and granting you its healing powers."

Arden sighed. "I see now why I'm being hunted."

"It's also the reason why the Or'Ackins attacked Elbrith eleven years ago. They believed the stone could undo their curse, so they decided to steal it. But even with their soul-charmed beings and the Grimstone in their hands, their army was far too small. So, they joined forces with Lord Zark, offering to share the Everstone's magic."

Zolan sat back down beside the boy.

"In the night, they attacked Elbrith. We were... unprepared," he said with grief.

"With an item of such power... didn't you expect someone to try and take it?" Arden asked, shaking his head.

"No. The Everstone was a secret, known only to the council of mages—or so we thought," Zolan said, raising a hand to his temple. "We foolishly took it for granted, and that's why Elbrith fell."

Arden remained silent. He envisioned the battle and all

the cruel moments those innocent people must've endured. He panned back down to his chest in ominous wonder.

The mage drew his attention to the Everstone as well. "They killed thousands, Arden... including your parents. I... I'm sorry."

The air left Arden's lungs, and he shut his eyes for a moment. Though he never knew his birth parents or thought of them much, an unexpected feeling of emptiness began to surface. He would never remember them nor meet them again. The hollow ache sank into his chest as if a piece of himself had been lost, a piece he didn't know was missing.

Zolan watched quietly. After a long pause, he spoke once more, his voice soft and filled with regret. "During the battle, an arrow pierced your chest." He reached out, pressing two gentle fingers onto the stone. "Right here... near your heart."

Arden didn't know how to respond. He could only listen.

"You were brought to the high mage just in time, who broke our council's vow and used the Everstone to heal you. But the stone did more than just seal your wound. It fused with your heart."

The boy looked on with even more confusion.

"But why?" he asked. "Why was the stone placed in me? I mean, I know I was injured, but why not someone else—someone more important?"

Zolan reached his hand for Arden's shoulder. "Because you are the nephew of the high mage... and now the last one alive in your bloodline."

CHAPTER 21

A KNOCK AT THE DOOR

Arden was speechless. He never imagined he'd be connected to a family of such high status. After all, he was just some poor thief living in a forest with nothing but a handful of chip to his name. How could *he* be so important?

Zolan gave the boy some time to settle into his new history, then said, "After the stone fused to your heart, I was ordered to take you away to Aramore in the hopes our enemies wouldn't find you.

While we managed to escape, the Or'Ackins must've unleashed the Grimstone's power in some way. From afar, a massive blue flash consumed the night sky, along with a horrendous quake that brought Elbrith to ruin."

The mage rubbed his chin.

Arden could sense the man was reliving the night in his head.

"I thought we were safe after that... but days later, my horse was shot with an arrow as we came upon a riverbend. We tumbled in, and you were taken by the current. I tried to save you, but an Or'Ackin sorcerer suddenly attacked me. I lost my hand during our battle. But with my remaining strength, I burned the sorcerer's face with one of my potions and sent him cowering back to Havarria."

Zolan hung his head, glaring at his hook hand.

"Everything that's happened to you is my fault," he muttered. "I-I failed you. I failed all of the Elves. I couldn't show my face in Aramore after that, so I banished myself to the desert to live with my guilt for losing you... and the Everstone."

The turmoil in the man's face grew. His eyes welled up with tears.

Arden sat with his thoughts, feeling the weight of Zolan's words sink in. It was hard to wrap his head around the idea that someone he'd just met had risked everything to save him. Yet, the deeper connection between them, forged through the stone and their shared past, felt undeniable. Zolan wasn't just a stranger—he was part of the reason Arden was still alive.

"Zolan, you tried, and for that, I'm grateful. If it wasn't for you, I wouldn't be here right now, and the stone would be with the Or'Ackins. Don't blame yourself for what they've done. You did what you could, and because of that, the stone is safer now than it would've been."

The mage gently cleared his throat with a slight cough, straightening his pose. "I guess you're right."

Arden nodded. "I have to say, though, this is going to be hard to convince Gord of."

Zolan agreed. "At least now you understand the weight of this situation."

"For the most part," said the boy. "But there is something else I'd like to know. The Or'Ackins... Surely, there must be some magic spells they could use to reverse their curse instead of taking the stone from me, right?"

Zolan shook his head. "The only true magic in this world comes from the stones. The Or'Ackins can soul-charm, yes, but that's due to how close they are to death. Living this way for so long has allowed their sorcerers to weaponize their curse. Rue'Na is one of these illusionists, chosen by the Or'Ackins to claim the Everstone. Her devotion to saving her kind from extinction fuels her pursuit of you."

"I see. And Zark?" Arden asked. "I assume he wants the stone for its power."

"Exactly. But in Zark's case, he believes the Or'Ackins owe him a debt and holds a dire need to prove his worth to Borka—a deity of the Dacarri. Gaining the stone would only further his agenda to conquer the eastern side. But regardless of these hunters' motives, we must protect the Everstone. Its fate lies with you, Arden."

Fate, the boy thought. A sudden reminder struck him. "Zolan, there's something else from the witch's prophecy I forgot to mention. She told me there's a beast to be defeated, a creature from beyond the grave that guards the heart of Death."

Zolan fell into a grim silence.

"She said it lies beneath ancestors' tomb," Arden continued. "What do you think she meant—"

Suddenly, a deep rumble shook the grand cavern.

"Did you feel that?" the boy asked.

Zolan nodded, looking around with curiosity.

Another quake boomed from behind the western wall of the cave. Dust filled the air as stalagmites fell from the ceiling, crashing into the gardens below.

Panic washed over Zolan's face.

"It's Zark," he gasped. "He's found us. We have to warn the others and get out of here. Now!"

Arden and the mage sprinted through the garden as the ground shook beneath their feet. They quickly ran to the staircase, surprised to see Vee and Buffoh already rushing toward them. Gord and Mugz followed shortly behind their trail.

"Is everyone alright?" the boy asked frantically.

"Yeah, kid. We're all fine," Buffoh replied, out of breath. "Where ya been this whole time?"

"And what's with all this rumbling?" Vee asked. "It sounds like the hill is coming down."

"It's Zark," Arden explained. "He knows we're here. We have to hurry."

"Oh, great!" Buffoh quipped sarcastically, shooting a glare at Zolan. "This is all your fault, ya know? With how fast that lunatic found us, we might as well have just stayed in the woods. This whole trip here was pointless, and so was that muck ya had me rub on my shoes, which—no thanks to *you*—are completely ruined."

Zolan scoffed. "If it wasn't for me, you'd be belly-up in those rapids right now, toad—"

"Stop!" Vee shouted. "We don't have time to fight. Getting out of here, *that's* what we need to do!"

"She's right," Arden agreed. "We need to find a way out. Zolan, you know this place better than any of us. Where do we go?"

Another boom resonated across the cave. A back wall in the garden began to quiver and crack.

"I'm thinking," Zolan said, pondering for a moment as a cold sweat trickled down his face. "The last time I was here, I left the same way we entered and crawled my way back up that winding tunnel we fell from. But that's no good now. There isn't enough time to reach it, let alone climb it. Zark's bull-pigs will be too fast to outrun."

Buffoh growled, "So now what? Do we just wait for that horn-headed maniac to come bargin' in here and kill us all? I ain't goin' out like that!"

Everyone grew somber as the Leptoid's words sank in.

Zolan snapped his fingers. "You may be onto something."

Buffoh's annoyed expression shifted to an anxious one. "Huh? Wait, I don't actually *want* him to kill us."

"No, not that part," Zolan clarified. "I mean, waiting for Zark to break in. If we allow him to collapse the cave wall, we just might be able to sneak by and escape through the opening he creates. Once outside, we can travel west. I know of a secret path through the woods so overgrown and narrow that Zark will never be able to get his bull-pigs through. That should put enough distance between us, and we can probably lose him for good."

It was a rather risky suggestion, but the group had no alternatives.

"So, what do we do?" Arden asked. "Just wait here?"

Zolan tapped his chin in thought. "No. Let's gather where Zark is breaking in. If we hide in the gardens nearby, we can avoid his stampede of knights as they enter the cave. By the time they charge inside and search for us, we'll have hopefully escaped. And if not... Well, then, I still have a few tricks up my sleeve."

Agreeing with the mage's plan, the group hurried through the gardens near the cracking wall and concealed themselves behind the shrubs. Anxiously, they waited as another quake shook the cavern. More rocks along the walls began to crumble and fall.

Mugz scurried onto Arden's shoulder, and the boy patted her on the head.

"Get ready, all of you!" Zolan shouted.

The hillside trembled again, and a sliver of daylight began to seep through the widening cracks. The weary travelers waited, trembling with adrenaline.

The feeling of impending doom filled the air as the muffled sound of chants and hooves snuck through the wall. The crashing grew louder and louder. Each thud shook the soil beneath them, sending a chill down Arden's spine.

Then there was a sudden pause in quaking, and the travelers looked at one another with concern.

Buffoh meekly turned to Zolan. "Do ya think they—"

BOOM!

The blinding light of the sunset illuminated the cavern. Rocks and stones tumbled into the room, shaking the ground violently. From behind the dusty plume that filled the cave, the trampling of bull-pigs approached. The Dacarri knights trudged over the boulders as they entered the chamber, wielding their swords and shouting with pride.

Luckily, not a single one of them had noticed the travelers hiding in the gardens.

"Now's our chance," Zolan yelled in a whisper to Arden and his friends. "Run!"

They bolted toward the newly opened wall of Dwyn. Vee and Gord quickly squeezed through, then Zolan. Arden followed after, but just as he was about to exit, he heard a desperate voice cry out from behind.

"Damn it! Wait, kid—I'm stuck! I'm stuck!"

Arden spun around. Buffoh was still caught in the entrance, his foot wedged tightly between two large rocks.

The boy rushed back. "Hold on, Buffoh!"

"What are you doing?" Zolan whispered sharply.

His pulse racing, Arden grabbed the Leptoid's shoulders, pulling with all his might.

"Hurry, kid. They're gonna spot us!" Buffoh said.

With a grunt, Arden wrenched the man free from the rocks. Buffoh stumbled forward, trying to gain his balance but the boy shoved him through the cave's opening anyway.

As they darted toward the light, their long shadows stretched against the floor, catching the attention of Zark's troops.

"They're escaping!" one of the soldiers cried out.

Without hesitation, the knights steered their mounts back toward the broken wall and began to charge.

Zolan rushed up beside Arden, his eyes scanning the threat.

"I'll take care of this!" he shouted. "Head west."

The boy and his companions fled while Zark's forces began to close in on Zolan. The brutish knights rallied forth, raising their stone blades.

Just as the soldiers approached, Zolan grabbed a vial from his side and hurled it at the ground beneath the bull-pigs' feet.

The glass shattered with a sharp crack, releasing an emerald flame that roared into a great wall, igniting the rocky entrance of Dwyn. The heat seared the air, filling the cavern with the pungent smell of burning herbs.

Blinded by the flash, the Dacarri knights were tossed from their scorched mounts, landing against all manner of trees and rocks nearby. Those still trapped inside the cave pulled their steeds backward, away from the fires that blocked the exit.

Zolan took the chance to retreat and made his way back to Arden and the others, eventually reuniting with them in the woods.

"What kind of potion was that?" Arden asked as the mage caught up to him.

"Not important," Zolan said. "Keep running. The pass is up ahead."

They continued forward, sprinting as fast as they could toward a sharp bend in the forest.

As they rounded the corner, they froze in their tracks. Blocking their way stood a towering man with giant antlers. It was Zark. The tyrant's ax blazed with flames as he charged atop a bull-pig, growling with rage.

Behind the scared travelers, the Dacarri knights, now free from Zolan's potion, rushed forth with swords held high.

Just as Lord Zark and his knights closed in, Zolan seized another vial from his belt and slammed it down. In an instant, a dark cloud exploded through the air, knocking everyone to their backs as it concealed the forest in a thick smoke.

Chapter 22

THE LOOMING STORM

As Arden hit the ground, Mugz toppled off his shoulder. The boy tried to open his eyes, but the ashy fumes burned like sand. Squinting through the pain, he could see only indistinct shadows moving about in the haze. Their shapes were blurred in the murky light. Arden tried to distinguish friend from foe, but it was nearly impossible. The only clear figure was Zark, his fiery ax slicing through the air as he roared in frustration.

The clamor of the Dacarri forces rang in the boy's ears as they screamed and stumbled about, colliding with each other in the sudden turn of events. But through the chaos, Arden could hear a familiar voice.

"Run, Arden!" Zolan shouted.

Arden climbed to his feet and dashed through the smoke. He couldn't tell which direction he was headed, but he did his best to avoid the trees and knights in his path.

Finally, he emerged from the fog and reached a clearing on a jagged cliffside. Sure, he had made it out in one piece, but there was nowhere else to run except back through the smoke.

Torn between finding his friends or waiting for them to emerge from the cloud, Arden stayed put, but horrors filled his thoughts. What if his companions were in danger and needed his help? What if they ran south and escaped Zark and the knights without him?

The weight of the guilt pressed down on the boy. He had

abandoned his own family in the chaos, leaving them to fend for themselves against Zark and his brutal forces. Images of his friends flashed through his mind: Buffoh's sarcastic remarks, Vee's determined gaze, Mugz's loyalty, and Gord's silent strength.

Reason eventually outweighed his fears, but before he could build up the courage to head back into the forest, the sound of bull-pigs approached. The heavy, rhythmic pounding of their hooves sent a shiver down his neck. In a panic, Arden took cover behind one of the few trees lining the cliff's edge.

Taking a moment to catch his breath, Arden looked across the cliffside toward the sea. A dark cloud had begun to block the sunset's dying rays. The stir of the nearing tempest matched the nervous grumbling in his stomach.

The sky darkened ominously, and the wind began to pick up, carrying with it the scent of rain and the promise of a storm.

Suddenly, a deep and intimidating voice shouted from the woods, "I know you're there, boy!"

Zark stepped into the clearing atop his bull-pig, surveying the area.

Arden crouched down, staying as still as he could.

"You can't cower away forever," the tyrant yelled. "Especially if you wish to see your friends again."

Zark snapped his fingers.

Commander Tull and the fourteen remaining knights emerged from the thinning smoke. Some rode atop their mounts while others dragged the boy's allies out from the shadows of the forest.

Arden snuck a glance, his heart sinking at the sight of his friends and family bound in rope, their mouths gagged.

An uncontrollable rage surged through him, and his fists curled.

"Listen closely, boy. This is your last chance," Zark said, scanning the cliffside. "I'm willing to offer you a deal. Hand over that stone, and I will set everyone free. But choose to deny me, and they will perish to the fires of my ax. So, who shall it be? You... or them?"

Arden struggled to find his courage. He wanted nothing more than to see his companions released, but terror kept him paralyzed. All he could do was watch from afar.

"So be it," Zark sneered, dismounting his bull-pig. "It seems the boy lacks the will to save these fools. Bring them to their knees!"

The soldiers yanked the prisoners down into the mud with brutal force. Gord erupted into a fit of rage, desperately struggling against his bindings.

"Control that beast!" Zark yelled.

A knight struck Gord's head with the handle of their stone sword. The Ogre's eyes fluttered in pain, and he was pulled back to the ground.

"That's better," Zark said. He walked over to the captives, gazing down at them carefully. "Who is it, Arden? Who is the one?"

The cruel tyrant held his ax in front of Vee's face, a deep hatred in her eyes as she stared at the man who killed her parents.

Zark shook his head, then moved to Zolan. The mage stayed firm, giving no expression.

"No," Zark whispered, making his way to Buffoh and Mugz next. The two shook with dread as the brute approached. Bellowing a quick chuckle at their pathetic display, he continued down the line to the last prisoner, Gord.

Zark peered down at Arden's father with a mocking frown. The Ogre scrunched his face in rage as he looked deep into the warrior's heartless eyes.

Zark smirked, then turned grim. "The worms can have *you* first."

Arden watched from behind the tree. Though his anger boiled, it wasn't enough to thaw his frozen body.

"Borka, father of all Dacarri," Zark cried, raising his weapon to the sky. "Grant me the fire of your might. Alight this ax with your fury!"

An orange light engulfed the woods as the ax went up in flames. Zark held its blades high above Gord's head.

Arden clutched the dirt at his feet. The thought of what came next burst him out of the immobilizing fear.

"Stop!" he yelled.

Zark held his ax steady. The blades' flames extinguished, wisping a gray smoke into the air. He turned back toward the cliffs. There stood the boy, his stark silhouette against the setting sun and the rolling storm behind him.

"I'll give you the stone," Arden said. "Just let them go, and you can have it. I won't resist."

Gord's large brow slowly sunk, and a tear dripped down his green cheek.

Zolan managed to free his mouth from the cloth gag. "No, Arden!" he yelled before shifting his focus to Zark. "Please, I'm begging you. Don't do this. We don't know what could happen—"

"Silence him!" shouted the antlered man.

The knights grabbed the spit-soaked cloth from the dirt and tied it around Zolan's head once more.

"Now," Lord Zark said in a much calmer tone, gazing back at the boy. "The stone."

Arden's tongue went dry as sand, and his fingers trembled as if pricked by pins and needles. He could hardly untie the strings of his shirt but managed to loosen a few. Before everyone's eyes, he exposed the stone.

Zark advanced toward him with a steady stride.

"Wait," Arden said, his voice beginning to crack. "At least let me say goodbye to my friends first—"

The tyrant slammed the boy down into the dirt with a heavy kick.

A sharp burst of air fled Arden's lungs as his back was harshly met with the cold dirt. A deep ache throbbed through his ribs, but all he could focus on was Zark's menacing stare.

"No more waiting," the man said, fixated on the sight of the Everstone. He pressed his heel against Arden's torso with immense strength. Then, with a terrible cry, he drove the finest point of Borka's ax down—straight into the boy's scarred chest.

A searing pain, more intense than anything Arden had ever imagined, overwhelmed him. Empty screams tore from his throat as a high-pitched tone rang in his ears, drowning out Zark's roar. His fingers curled into the soil, squeezing clumps of grass so tightly that his knuckles turned white.

Just then, the Everstone began to glow as intensely as the sun. The nearby bull-pigs shrieked, their hooves scraping against the ground in a wild frenzy. Arden clenched his eyes shut against the pain, but the piercing light of the stone shined through.

Zark raged at the stone's refusal to be pried from the boy's chest, his growl deepening as he pressed his ax harder and harder.

Arden writhed in agony, but a sudden roar thundered from above, and the pressure of Zark's blade vanished. The boy gasped, his lungs finally able to draw in the air again. The intense relief left him dizzy as the glow of the Everstone began to dim, then fade away entirely.

The boy slowly opened his eyes through a veil of sweat, blinking to clear his vision. At first, everything was a blur, shapes, and shadows swirling about, but eventually, he realized Zark was no longer standing above him.

A loud snarl to the left caught Arden's attention.

There, just beside the edge of the cliff, Rue'Na sat atop her gringore, its heavy claws tossing the Dacarri lord around with ease.

Zark wedged the handle of his ax between the powerful jaws of the beast. Angered, the creature latched on and flailed its head, violently dragging the man through the mud.

As Rue'Na launched her attack, Arden witnessed a wave of chaos sweep over the Dacarri. The knights scattered about, yelling to one another as their startled bull-pigs fled for the forest. Commander Tull raised her sword, poised to enter the fight. For a moment, it looked like she was about to aid Zark against the gringore, but then she stopped.

Arden watched as hesitation stalled her every movement. Tull stared at the battlefield, her grip on her hilt loosening. Slowly, she stepped back and thrust her sword into the ground.

"What are you doing?" a passing soldier shouted in frustration.

"This isn't right," Tull called back, her voice carrying across the clamor. "This isn't what we stand for."

The soldier hesitated, then shook his head in disbelief

and ran toward Zark to assist.

Tull remained steadfast.

From afar, Arden couldn't tell if it was courage or fear that rooted her in place.

Suddenly, he moved his focus onto Zolan, struggling in the dirt from the corner of his eye. The mage broke free from his bindings and gave the boy a nod, staying low as he quietly moved toward Gord and the others. Then, with a careful slice of his hook, he freed their bound hands and mouths.

The Dacarri knights shouted with fury as they noticed their prisoners escaping.

"Quick! Don't let them get away!" a soldier barked.

The other troops charged for the mage, their swords raised.

Zolan reached for his satchel and began hurling various potions into the crowd of soldiers. Some vials erupted into billowing clouds of ash, while others burst forth a sticky tar, ensnaring the knights' feet to the ground.

One of the warriors headed straight for Buffoh, who snatched a shield from the ground with his long tongue and held it up to defend himself.

Mugz growled, frantically scratching and clawing at any knight she could.

Vee hastily grabbed a fallen soldier's sword and rushed into the fray. The girl's movements were swift and precise, the blade an extension of her wrath. With revenge burning in her bloodshot eyes, she made way for Zark.

Arden, still feeling faint from the Dacarri lord's attempt at removing the Everstone, stumbled to his feet. The boy rubbed his eyes at the mayhem unfolding before him. As he turned to his side, he caught a glimpse of the Or'Ackin sorceress atop her gringore, still struggling in its tussle with Zark.

Rue'Na snapped her head to the side with a sharp crack as if sensing Arden's gaze. Her white eyes locked onto him, peering into his soul. With a swift strike of her whip, she commanded the gringore's attention, drawing it to their new target. The beast gave Zark one final swipe, knocking the man to the ground before charging at Arden next.

The young Elf tripped over his feet but managed to snag an abandoned spear before scrambling for the cover of the woods. In the distance, the gringore barreled behind him, its massive limbs plowing through the thickets.

As Arden fled from Rue'Na and her gringore, night had fallen, and the looming storm was almost upon them. A terrible lightning struck the forest, strobing against the trees in a series of blinding flashes. The tempest's fury grew more intense with each passing second.

Arden knew he had to keep moving and use the forest's natural cover to his advantage. He darted through the underbrush, his breath coming in quick gasps.

Suddenly, a low snarl rumbled closer than he expected. Arden spun on his heel, gripping the wooden spear he'd acquired.

The beast emerged from the dark, its rotting teeth glinting by the flicker of a distant lightning strike.

Terror surged through Arden's veins, every instinct screaming for him to flee. Yet, as the gringore prowled closer, something deep within him pushed back. He thought of the countless times he had run from this huntress—how she and her mount always seemed too close no matter how far he fled. The boy clenched his jaw and tightened his grip on the spear.

Not this time, he told himself. *This ends here.*

The beast lunged forward, its muscles rippling beneath its bristling fur. Arden quickly sidestepped, thrusting the spear forward into the gringore's flank. The beast let out a bone-rattling roar as it staggered about.

Arden's heart leaped—he had wounded it! A small glimmer of triumph surged in his chest, but the victory was fleeting. The gringore twisted violently, swinging a massive claw through the air. Arden barely had time to react as the beast snapped his spear in half.

The boy's eyes fell on the broken weapon—its jagged edge speaking to both his success and sudden misfortune. But the battle left no time for hesitation.

With a determined face, Arden raised the severed spear high and hurled it at the creature with all his strength.

The splintered wood slammed into the gringore's right paw with a sickening thud. The beast let out a guttural snarl, thrashing in fury.

Without a second thought, Arden turned and bolted through the woods.

Rue'Na snapped her whip through the air, cracking it with great force against the gringore's side.

"Get after him! You worthless thing!" she snarled, pushing the creature back into pursuit.

The gringore limped through branches and roots to reach its prey, but Arden was swift. Weaving between the trees, his slender frame slipped through the gaps, granting him distance. Then, like a shadow, the Elf vanished from Rue'Na's view and took refuge behind some rocks near the edge of the forest.

Snarling in frustration, the sorceress slowed her injured mount and scanned the surroundings, her watchful eye passing over every stick and stone.

"You won't evade me again, Elf!" she hissed. "I will bring you to Havarria in pieces if I must."

Arden waited behind the rocks, listening closely for the gringore's heavy steps, taking the chance to catch his breath as quietly as he could. The beast sounded further off, allowing him enough time to conjure up some sort of escape. Glancing through the trees and down a hill just ahead, the boy could see a cliff, its stark edge dropping straight down toward the sea.

The boy placed a hand on the ground, getting a feel for the slippery mud. Recalling that the huntress was tethered to her steed with swamp vines, an idea formed in his mind. He mustered up the courage to execute his plan, then leaped out into the open.

"Rue'Na!" he shouted through the woods. "I know what you really are!"

The woman spun her head toward the sound, her mount coming to an abrupt halt. She spotted the boy in the distance, leering at his dark silhouette.

"You're cursed! Soulless!" Arden yelled. "You call yourself a sorceress, but all you have are illusions—tricks. And once the Grimstone's power has killed all of your kind, the Or'Ackins will become nothing more than a myth—just a frightening tale for children. So come and claim my stone if you wish, but I doubt it can even save you now."

Rue'Na's glare widened, and her lips twitched, revealing her ashen teeth. A deafening crack resounded as she whipped her steed and let out a blood-curdling scream. The gringore rushed forward as she threw her searing-hot boomerang for the boy.

Arden jumped to the side, barely avoiding the blade as it zipped past his head. He rolled to his feet, ready to dodge the oncoming gringore, hoping it might slide down the muddy hill and off the cliff's edge. But as he prepared to make his move, a faint whirring sound approached from behind.

A scorching pain sliced across Arden's shoulder as Rue'Na's boomerang returned to her hand. The boy fell to the ground, clutching his arm as he tumbled to the base of the hill.

The gringore licked its scarred lips, eyeing Arden's injury. As it closed in on the boy, Rue'Na yanked hard on the beast's reins. With a fierce thrust of its hind legs, the creature lunged forward, claws outstretched and jaws agape—ready for the strike.

With no time to move, Arden braced for the sharp pain of the gringore's bite.

Suddenly, a massive boulder tore through the air and struck the beast with great force. The impact sent the creature spiraling. Its roar was cut short as it lifelessly crashed beside Arden and slid toward the cliff's edge.

The boy watched as Rue'Na frantically thrashed against the vines binding her to the defeated gringore. She wrenched at them with all her might, but the roots tightened with her every struggle. Arden could only make out her wild movements as she violently swung her boomerang. For the first time, he realized the weight of her desperation—heard it in her cries of rage. This was her last, futile attempt to save herself and the Or'Ackins from doom.

Arden felt the faintest touch of sympathy arise, but it was too late. Before the sorceress could free herself, the beast's dead weight pulled her over the cliff.

The boy held his breath as she vanished in a heart-stopping moment of silence. Then—

A thunderous splash erupted from below the cliff, and the forest fell quiet once more.

Rue'Na was gone.

Arden let out a tired sigh, feeling his tense muscles unwind. He turned toward the source of the mysterious boulder, spotting his father amidst the trees. The Ogre's massive green arms pulsed, drooping with exhaustion.

"Gord!" Arden exclaimed, his breath easing.

The Ogre stumbled over to his son, scooping him up from the ground in a tight embrace.

For a precious moment, the memory of battle faded into the background, and in the warm hold of his father, Arden found a quiet reassurance—a reminder, that even amidst the chaos, there was love and hope.

Continuing to press his face into the man's torso, the boy said, "I thought I was done for."

Gord released him, then signed, *Not as long as I'm still around.*

Arden smiled, wiping the tears from his cheek. He took a moment to clear his throat, staring off to where Rue'Na fell.

"You saved me," Arden said quietly, his voice thick with gratitude. "I don't know what I would've done without you."

Gord placed a hand on his son's shoulder, squeezing it gently.

You're stronger than you know, he signed. *But I'll always be here when you need me, son. No matter what.*

Arden smiled, letting those words settle into his heart before looking back at the cliff.

"Do you think Rue'Na is still alive?"

Gord looked out to the sea in wonder, then slowly shook his head. He faced his son with a smirk.

Arden felt relief, but the peace quickly shifted as Gord's stare narrowed, his eyes fixed on something in the distance.

"What is it?" Arden asked with concern as he too drew attention to the south.

A warm light flickered between the trees up ahead, its orange glow hovering just above the forest. The radiance spread as if growing with each passing second.

Without another word, Arden and his father hurried toward the edge of the cliff to investigate. As they walked down the muddy slope, a horrifying sight came into view. The southern forest was engulfed in flames, smolders of ash billowing high into the storm clouds above.

A *blaze like that could only mean one thing*, Arden thought.

"Zark," the boy whispered gravely.

CHAPTER 23

THROUGH FIRES OF MIGHT

Vee ran through the smoldering woods with Zark hot on her trail. They had strayed far to the west, away from the battlefield. Not an echo resounded from the squeal of a bull-pig, nor the chant of a Dacarri knight. Now, only the crackle of sparks and hiss of flames filled the air.

Dozens of tree trunks bore the brutal marks of the tyrant's ax, bleeding hot sap like fresh wounds. Amidst the devastation, sanctuaries remained in the form of timbers untouched by Zark's blade.

Vee sought refuge behind one of the trees, pressing herself against its warm bark.

Lord Zark arrived shortly after, his hefty footsteps thudding in the dirt as his pace slowed to a steady beat.

"I should have killed you when I had the chance," he growled. "You bring shame to all of Dacarr and to Borka's great name. You will not escape his fires again."

Vee shut her eyes tightly, wishing it would all end as his menacing voice grew closer.

"You're just like them—your family. Weak. A spineless coward," Zark said, circling every unburned tree he passed. "*They*, at least, had the bravery to face me. But you? Hah! You run and hide... just like the child you still are, Delvina."

The girl clenched her fists, his words cutting like knives to her heart. She ached to say something back—to defend her honor—but held her tongue instead.

Zark's voice suddenly fell silent, his footsteps fading away.

Vee held her breath, glancing from side to side. Not a sound followed to signify the man was still nearby. All she could hear was the roar of distant flames climbing up the walls of the forest behind her.

The girl braved a step to the left, peeking out to see if the tyrant had gone. To her surprise, there was no one. She sighed, closing her eyes for a moment of peace. But then, A deep war cry bellowed from her right, prompting the girl to duck down. Zark's ax plunged into the bark above her head, practically cleaving the tree in two. Vee rolled forward to dodge the burst of flames as the timber was set alight. She darted for the woods ahead as fast as her legs could carry her.

Zark flailed his weapon about, striking the trees while he sprinted behind, barely missing the girl with each powerful swing.

Before long, Vee found herself encircled by a violent ring of fire, for she'd somehow doubled back to an area still ablaze. She held her chest as a bitter smoke filled the air.

Zark emerged around the opposite end of the fiery ring, his figure obscured by the choking smog.

Vee watched in terror, images of her nightmare from the swamp flashing across her mind. Her pursuit from the fire giant was no hallucination but a premonition. It was a glimpse into her very future, a vision of her death.

A sarcastic chuckle left the antlered man's throat as the blades of his ax extinguished.

"You will never avenge anyone," he said. "By my hand, you'll die here. This forest shall be your tomb!"

Zark charged ahead.

Vee raised her stone sword high to block the tyrant's blow, but Zark's ax came down with devastating force, knocking the blade clean from her grasp. The sword flew through the air, spinning wildly before vanishing into the surrounding fire.

Defenseless, she fell to her knees, her last drop of courage snuffed out as she anxiously scanned the blistering inferno. The girl's chest fell short of air, her sweaty brow turning deathly cold as she peered into Zark's blazing eyes.

The man raised his ax high, but his gaze darted out to the scorched forest around them. As the blackened trees began to crumble nearby, his grip on the ax loosened.

For just a mere moment, Vee saw something shift within him—a far-off whisper of doubt. But just as quickly as it had appeared, his uncertainty vanished.

Zark snapped back down to her.

"I call to you, Borka, father of all Dacarri!" he screamed, aiming his weapon above Vee's head. "Grant me the fire of your might."

A snapping sound echoed from behind him.

"Alight this ax with your fury so I may purge the world of your enemies forever!" he shouted.

Vee's eyes grew wide as a tree that Zark had sliced earlier cracked in half and came swooping down toward them both. With her final bout of strength, she rolled out of the way, barely dodging the tyrant's deadly swing.

The tree came tumbling down, and with it, the deafening sound of a thousand breaking branches. The ground shook with a terrible quake, and Zark's chanting was cut short.

Suddenly, all was still.

Vee gasped for air, her back pressed against the ground

as a cloud of ash billowed into the trees. She staggered to her feet, squinting through the dense haze, fearing that Zark might still be lurking somewhere in the gloom. But the scene before her told a different story.

The massive fallen tree stretched out ahead, its heavy trunk pinning Zark's lifeless body beneath it. Only his hand was visible, jutting out from under the charred bark, still gripping Borka's ax tightly.

Without warning, a heavy downpour erupted from the storm clouds above, drenching the forest in a torrent of rain. Each droplet cut through the thick smog, washing away the remnants of destruction. The once-raging fires that engulfed the surrounding trees sputtered and dwindled into nothing more than a light smolder.

Minutes passed, and soon the storm began to tire itself out. As the remaining smoke dissipated, Vee stood before the charred tree at her feet, its damp bark sizzling. The girl's war with Zark had finally come to an end. The tyrant was dead.

An emptiness began to creep into Vee's heart, a hollowness that gnawed at her soul. She had exacted her revenge, but it brought no satisfaction—only sorrow for the things she couldn't undo.

Vee collapsed to her knees in exhaustion. She hung her head, pressing her face into the palms of her cold hands.

The heavy stride of footsteps suddenly drew near, breaking the girl from her solitude.

Peeking through the gaps between her fingers, Vee watched as Commander Tull entered the clearing. The woman's bark armor hardly bore a scratch, as if she hadn't partaken in the battle at all. Despite having no visible injuries, her gait conveyed weariness, as though she'd spent hours scouring the woods. Tull's eyes fixed on Vee, then quickly moved to Zark's body under the fallen tree.

The woman remained silent as she strode over to Borka's ax, grasping it from the mud. Emotionless, she marched for the girl, wielding the weapon firmly in her hands.

Vee's energy was utterly spent, leaving her incapable of fleeing.

Tull's face turned steely as she raised the ax to her side.

"For so many years, I blindly followed Zark," the woman said. "He claimed he was acting in Borka's name—for the good of Dacarr. But somewhere along the way, I realized it was a lie."

Vee took a deep breath.

"Why didn't you try to stop him?" she asked bluntly.

"Because I was mindlessly loyal to our corrupt kingdom. I couldn't find the strength to vanquish Zark on my own. And now, after all these years of manipulation, our soldiers have lost sight of their true purpose. Instead of fighting for our people, they've naively fought in the name of Zark. If I had tried to stop this myself, I would've been executed for treason, and Zark's agenda might have endured anyway."

The Commander clenched her jaw, staring at the ax in her palm. "His failure had to come by his own hand."

Vee's fears subsided as she realized Tull was not driven by anger but by the haunting guilt of her own choices.

"So... you're not going to kill me?" the girl asked wearily.

"No," Tull replied, lowering the weapon as she glared back at Zark's hand. "And if it brings you any solace, our pursuit for the stone is over. It doesn't belong to the Dacarri. It never did."

With a sense of pride, the Commander knelt and placed

the ax on the ground in front of Vee. "You possess the bravery I've always longed for—an undying fire. Never lose it."

Vee looked at the weapon with confusion.

"You don't want it?" she asked.

Tull arose, her stare blank. "That thing has brought our kingdom nothing but despair. It hasn't been a symbol of hope in a very long time. And now, with Zark defeated, I can bring Dacarr back to order and reform it to what it was really about... each other."

The Commander gave a nod, then began to walk east.

"Wait!" Vee said, glancing down at the ax. "What am I supposed to do with this?"

Tull stopped in her tracks. "Do whatever you please. I'm returning to Dacarr with the remaining knights. If you wish to come back home, you'll still have a place among us—that is, if you want it."

Vee shook her head. "There's nothing left for me there."

The Commander smirked. "Good luck to you, Delvina."

Arden and Gord entered the clearing, their eyes sweeping over the scorched landscape, searching desperately for any sign of their friends. The devastation left by the fire was overwhelming, but a wave of relief washed over them as they spotted Vee. She was kneeling beside a toppled tree, her focus drawn solely to Borka's ax.

Gord turned to his son, his expression serious as he signed, *I'll find the others. You go on ahead.*

Arden nodded, then cautiously made his way toward the girl.

As he approached, the boy noticed Zark's hand protruding from beneath the fallen tree. For a moment, he felt a great peace, knowing the tyrant had finally come to an end. He glanced at Vee, expecting to see a shimmer of triumph in her eyes, but instead saw only despair.

Arden knelt beside her, gazing at the charred timber in front of them.

Vee exhaled a heavy breath, then said, "I've been consumed by hatred for so long that I failed to see how killing Zark would make me any different than him. Now that he's gone, I don't feel any better. My family is still dead either way."

"But what about your sister in Haroon?" Arden asked. "You said that she—"

"Zark took her too," Vee replied, her voice trembling. She grabbed the amber pendant around her neck and held it toward the boy. "This is all I have left of her."

A tear trickled down her cheek.

"Vee, I... I had no idea. I'm so sorry."

"Don't be. I chose not to tell you. Admitting she's gone would've made it more real. But I guess that's because... it *is* real."

Arden remained silent, letting the girl gather her thoughts.

Vee cleared her throat, then said, "When I learned from the other rebels that Zark was leaving Dacarr, I knew it was the perfect time to get my revenge. I snuck aboard his ship and hid in the cellar for over a week until the night that we arrived at Mogoroth Bay. The troops set up a camp in the woods, and I found Zark alone in his tent, asleep. I drew my dagger, held it above his chest..."

Arden watched as the girl clenched her fist, thrusting it into the dirt.

"I wanted so much to bring that blade down, but something inside me just couldn't do it. In my moment of weakness, Zark woke up and sliced my leg with his ax. Somehow, I escaped, but I feared he was going to hunt me down. I couldn't risk being associated with the Dacarri, so I filed my horns and posed as an Elf."

Vee parted the left side of her hair, uncovering a scarred patch where a small antler had once grown. Now reduced to a rugged stump, it was coated with dried blood that blended in with her hair.

Arden shook his head, feeling a deep well of empathy, wishing he could help Vee bear the weight of her grief.

The girl continued, "Days later, I stumbled upon Rook and got directions to the nearest city, Haroon. But I got lost trying to find my way there, and instead, I found you."

Vee's lips curled into a gentle smirk. "So, I guess it wasn't *all* bad."

The boy smiled back at her, and together, they enjoyed a moment of silence.

Arden glanced around, taking in the sights of the smoldering woods. His eyes drifted over to Borka's ax, sparking a question on his mind.

"So, what are you going to do with it?" he asked.

"I don't know," Vee said frankly. "It's such a dark reminder—and not just of my own past—but of all those who fell to its blades. Keeping it would only haunt me. Perhaps no one should have it."

Arden mused.

"I think I can help with that," he finally said. The boy stood up and held an inviting hand toward the girl. "Come on."

Vee grabbed hold of him and pulled herself to her feet.

Together, they lifted the ax from the ground, its handle still warm to the touch. Arden guided the way toward the edge of a cliff nearby. Then, side by side, the two companions held the weapon out toward the ocean below.

"Ready?" Arden asked.

"Wait," Vee said, her voice fragile against the growing wind. She glared at the ancient weapon one last time, its history etched into every crevice of the stone blades. A shaky breath left her throat. "Let's do it."

With a powerful swing, they sent the ax plummeting down. It struck the water with a resounding splash, then descended into the abyss, leaving only gentle ripples atop the surface.

Arden turned to Vee.

The girl watched the rising sun with uncertainty in her eyes.

"I don't know my purpose anymore," she said softly. "I've spent years wanting this, and now... I'm not sure what comes next for me. I can't go back to Dacarr. With my family gone, it hasn't felt like home in a long time. I'm not even sure what home means to me anymore."

Arden looked to the sky, its familiar rays reminiscent of the mornings he and Gord would watch the sunrise from the cliffs of Noakwood Hollow.

"Gord once told me that home isn't a place. It's the people you care about—the ones who will always stand by your side, no matter the distance. After losing almost everything, I finally understood what he meant. I took my family and friends for granted, thinking that shiny necklaces and fancy beds would make me happy. But true happiness comes from the people who make you feel at home, like you."

A grin peeked from Vee's lips, and she gave a small chuckle. "Gord's pretty sentimental, huh?"

Arden laughed. "I suppose he is."

"So, this Noakwood Hollow place of yours... Do you think I'd like it?"

The boy turned to her, his eyes alight. "Well, it's probably nothing like Dacarr, but the springtime there *is* quite beautiful. I should warn you, though, Gord's cooking... it's awful."

"I'll be the judge of that," Vee snickered.

The two of them shared a laugh, then headed toward the forest in search of their friends.

While traveling east, Arden observed the woodland floor as they came to an area left unscorched by Zark's fire. The ground was scattered with stone swords, and various potions dripped from the trees.

In the distance, Buffoh sat atop a massive stump, slouched over and tying a bindle to a stick. Gord rested near a cluster of rocks, picking the dirt from beneath his nails, while Mugz sat by his side, licking her fur. Zolan paced behind them, seemingly lost in thought.

Arden and Vee quickened their pace at the sight of their friends ahead.

As they approached, Buffoh's stare flew upward.

"Ay, kid! Ya made it!" he exclaimed. "We were worried

about ya. Are those hunters finally gone?"

Arden nodded with a new sense of hope in his eyes.

"Phew!" the Leptoid said, wiping the sweat from his forehead. "That's a relief. Ya should've seen this mage here. He was kickin' Dacarri butt like it was nothin'."

Zolan rolled his eyes but hid a grin. "Well, you weren't too bad out there yourself, toad."

Buffoh hopped down from the stump, straightening his clothes before lugging the packed bindle over his shoulder. "Well, it's been a wild ride, kid. Never thought I'd find myself in this kinda mess with a bunch of strangers. But I guess that's what life's all about, right? It's unpredictable."

The old Leptoid reached down and grabbed a sturdy stick to use as a walking cane.

"So, this is it? You're finally going?" Arden asked.

Gord and Vee turned to the Leptoid with curiosity.

Buffoh sighed and slowly looked around at the group, his eyes lingering on each member. There was a subtle hesitation in his usual riotous manner, and for a moment, the Leptoid seemed to weigh his decision. He glanced at Gord, then Vee, and finally Arden as if silently measuring the cost of leaving.

Scratching the back of his neck, Buffoh said, "Ay, kid, it was nice bein' in ya company, but ya don't need a guide like me anymore. And besides, I've got other matters to attend to back at Anura. I *do* have a shop to run, ya know? I should be headin' back."

"Oh," Arden replied with slight disappointment. "Right. Yes, I guess you should."

"Also, I think I left out some kibbler milk at home... I can only imagine how many legs that thing grew while I was away," Buffoh added with a joking tone.

Arden chuckled a bit as the Leptoid glanced around the group once more.

"Welp," he began, "take care, furball, lady, Ogre... You too, mage." He hobbled over to Arden. "Kid, thanks for showin' me a more *adventurous* side of life. I wish ya the very best of luck—and try not to get into any more trouble, will ya?"

The man threw out his hand for a shake.

Arden grasped it firmly, looking into the Leptoid's kind orange eyes. "You too, Buffoh. I'll miss you. Travel safe."

Buffoh smirked, then said with a deep sincerity, "Good-bye, Arden."

With a quick sniffle, he cleared his throat and turned eastward.

The boy watched as Buffoh began his journey home. There was something about his departure that left an emptiness in Arden's core—bittersweet and a little unexpected. For all his superstitions, complaints, and charges for every little thing, Buffoh had been a companion—a guide in more ways than one.

"Buffoh, wait!" the boy shouted. "What about the rest of the money I owe you?"

The old toad continued onward, his voice carrying back through the trees. "Don't worry about it, kid. Maybe there are more important things in my life than some chip."

Then, Buffoh disappeared into the dense woods. For a long time, Arden stood still, his thoughts a whirlwind as he stared at the spot where Buffoh had walked out of sight.

Vee's voice broke the silence, thoughtful and light.

"Do you think he'll be alright?" she asked, approaching the boy's side. "I mean, he *did* get us lost in the swamp... even with a map."

"He'll be fine," Arden reassured. "He's got his lucky gribic's eye with him."

Gord walked over to join them with Mugz perched lazily on his shoulder. The little creature yawned, clutching at the Ogre's shirt and gazing at Arden with sleepy eyes.

With a gentle tap on his son's shoulder, Gord signed, *Looks like we're down a member, but we'll manage. Honestly, it will be nice to finally have some peace and quiet.*

Arden sighed, the sadness of Buffoh's farewell lingering with him. He glanced back at Zolan, who'd been giving the travelers their space.

"True," Arden admitted. "But at least Zolan's here to keep us on track. He's done so much for us already. I think it's time we started trusting him more. Don't you?"

Gord's gaze flew to the mage, his expression softening as he signed back, *I agree. He's earned that much.*

Vee stepped forward, crossing her arms with a playful smirk. "So, Stoneheart, what now?"

Arden blinked, startled by the new name. "Stoneheart?"

"Yeah," Vee shrugged. "That's what I'm calling you from now on."

Arden mulled it over for a moment.

Stoneheart, he thought.

The title didn't feel too out of place. The weight of the Everstone and the constant responsibility he carried—it all seemed to fit with the name.

"I think I like that," he admitted, a smile tugging at his lips. "But just don't go around saying it in public, alright?"

"Obviously," Vee replied, grinning. "You think I want more people hunting us down? No thanks."

Arden chuckled again.

"But seriously," Vee added, her tone shifting to a more purposeful one, "where to now?"

Zolan walked over to join the group.

"The choice is yours," he said to the boy.

Arden's gaze wandered. His thoughts shifted to a place that had been with him all along—the place that felt like the heart of his journey. He looked at Gord, whose warm eyes reflected the same feelings as his own.

The cheerful Ogre signed gently, confirming the answer.

Vee watched them, her brow furrowing slightly as she observed the gesture.

"What did he say?" she asked curiously.

Arden's smile deepened. "Home."

www.ingramcontent.com/pod-product-compliance
Lightning Source LLC
Chambersburg PA
CBHW061119100726
47911CB00013B/602